Wishbone gasped and jumped up. "Joe! They're blaming the wrong guy! Tell them!"

"What's wrong, Joe?" David asked.

Taking a deep breath, Joe pushed the hair off his forehead. "I wasn't supposed to leave the house this afternoon and look for a camping site, so I did it while my mom was in town shopping. Curtis couldn't have been the one to write on the *Chronicle*'s windows—I saw him in the park at the time it happened."

"So why didn't you tell the truth?" David asked.

"If my mom finds out I went to the park, I'll probably get grounded. That'd mean good-bye camping trip. And after what Curtis did to us . . ."

"Bingo!" Wishbone said. "To save Curtis, you'd have to sacrifice yourself. That's a tough one."

The Adventures of WISHBONE™

DOG OVERBOARD!

by Vivian Sathre
Inspired by *Kidnapped*
by Robert Louis Stevenson

WISHBONE™ created by Rick Duffield

SCHOLASTIC INC.
New York Toronto London Auckland Sydney

ISBN 0-590-03093-0

12 11 10 9 8 7 6 5 4 3 2 1   9   8 9/9 0 1 2 3/0

Printed in the U.S.A.   40

Edited by Pam Pollack
Copy edited by Jonathon Brodman
Cover design by Lyle Miller
Interior illustrations by Don Punchatz
Wishbone photograph by Carol Kaelson

For Roger,

with special thanks

to the rest of my support team—

Karsten, Mitchell, Erika, Charlie, Virginia, and Bill

FROM THE BIG RED CHAIR . . .

Oh . . . hi! Wishbone here. You caught me right in the middle of some of my favorite things—books. Let me welcome you to THE ADVENTURES OF WISHBONE. In each of these books, I have adventures with my friends in Oakdale and imagine myself as a character in one of the greatest stories of all time. This story takes place in late summer, when Joe is thirteen and he and his friends are about to enter seventh grade—during the first season of my television show. In *DOG OVERBOARD!*, I imagine I'm a young boy named David Balfour, from Robert Louis Stevenson's adventure story *KIDNAPPED*. It's a great tale about friendship and how important it is to help someone who is facing incredible odds.

You're in for a real treat, so pull up a chair and a snack and sink your teeth into *DOG OVERBOARD!*

Chapter One

Wishbone jumped down from his big red chair the second he heard Joe turn off the cordless phone. He trotted out of the Talbots' study and into the living room, where Joe was sitting on the sofa, smiling. Wishbone wagged his tail. "Okay, pal. It's a warm, sunny Saturday. What's our plan for this afternoon? Something adventurous, right?"

Joe put the phone on the coffee table. He gave Wishbone a quick scratch behind the ears. Then he stood up.

"Mom?" Joe called, brushing past Wishbone as he headed toward the kitchen. "It's okay with David's parents—we can camp out in Jackson Park. But we have to do it tomorrow night instead of tonight. David's parents are going out tonight, and he has to watch his sister, Emily."

Wishbone trotted into the kitchen behind Joe. "Excuse me, but the dog was talking." He paced impatiently. "Helllooo! Remember me? Your best friend? About fourteen inches high, white, with a few perfectly placed brown and black spots?" Wishbone came up in front of Joe, then stopped. "What are we doing today? I think we still have time to dig a few holes before lunch." He waited a few seconds for Joe to respond. When Joe didn't say anything, Wishbone sighed. "No one ever listens to the dog."

Joe's mom, Ellen, looked up from the table, where she sat writing out a grocery list. "Camping tomorrow instead of tonight is probably a good thing, Joe. You've been promising for weeks to clean out the garage before the Oakdale Historical Society holds its rummage sale." She tilted her head. "Well, the sale is tomorrow. I need to take our donations over to the society's office before dinner tonight." Ellen turned her attention back to her list.

"I'll get to it, Mom." Joe plopped into a chair and looked hopefully at his mom. "It's just that right now David and I are going to bike over to Pepper Pete's. It's having a one-price, all-you-can-eat lunch to mark the end of summer."

Wishbone wagged his tail. "Count the dog in on this one." He looked at Ellen with his big brown eyes. "Ellen, oh, kind and generous one, loan me four bucks, would you?"

Suddenly Joe broke into a grin and switched subjects again. "Camping is going to be so much fun—just David and me."

"What about the dog?" Wishbone sat down directly in front of Joe and stared up at him.

"Oh, and Wishbone's going to be with us," Joe said, bending to pet him.

"Thank you, Joe." Relaxing under Joe's comforting hand, Wishbone looked at Ellen, who was top dog in the Talbot house. Not only was she nice, but she was in charge of the food—a good combination, any way you looked at it. "Need any help beefing up that list, Ellen?"

Ellen stood up, checked the canned-food cabinet, then wrote down more items on her list.

Joe got up and started to leave the room. "Come on, Wishbone, let's go get David. 'Bye, Mom."

"Wait." Ellen looked at her watch, then at Joe.

"Uh-oh, Joe. The 'mom' look." Wishbone put his head down and placed a paw over one eye.

"The day is slipping away, and you haven't even started cleaning out the garage." Ellen leaned against the kitchen counter. "I want you to come right home after lunch and spend the rest of the afternoon cleaning it out." She slipped her hands into her pants pockets. "Okay, Joe? Don't make any other plans for the day."

"But, Mom, David and I are going to pick out a campsite this afternoon."

"The garage needs to be done, Joe. Come home after lunch and take care of it. And if you have any extra time, you can check your room for clothes to donate to the sale." Turning, she added, "You have all day tomorrow to pick out your site."

Joe nodded. "Okay, Mom. I promise. I'll come straight home and work on the garage. It'll be done this afternoon."

"Thanks," Ellen said.

Joe got on his bike and rode across the cul-de-sac to the house that belonged to one of his best friends—David Barnes. Then he got off his bike, put down his kickstand, and ran onto the porch and rang the bell.

Wishbone took a minute to sniff along the Barneses' white picket fence before finally joining Joe at the door. "Maybe David's busy inventing something again," Wishbone said as they waited. "I don't know how someone going into the seventh grade can come up with so many good ideas."

Just then David wheeled his bike from behind the house.

"There you are," Joe said, jumping off the porch and getting back on his bike. "I was beginning to wonder—"

"I was out back," David said.

Wishbone followed the boys as they zigged up one street and zagged down another one. After awhile, they reached Pepper Pete's Pizza Parlor.

"Boy, the line is clear out the door," David said, as they slid their bikes into the rack nearby.

Joe sighed. "So I see. But at least it's moving."

"Speaking of moving," Wishbone said, "let's go, guys!" He trotted off ahead of Joe and David and got them a place in line.

"I'm really excited about camping tomorrow night," Joe said.

"Me, too," David said, as the threesome moved ahead with the rest of the line. "Can you believe school starts in a few days?"

"Not really," Joe said. "It seems like summer just started."

Wishbone sniffed the air, enjoying the strong pizza smell. "Mmm-mmm. Hey, wait a minute." He poked his nose higher into the air. "I smell something . . . Damont." Wishbone turned and looked back. Two boys in denim shorts and striped T-shirts approached. "Oh, it's Damont and his sidekick, Curtis. As always, my nose knows."

The two classmates of Joe and David stopped and smiled as if they were old friends.

"Well, what do ya know," Damont said, slapping Joe on the back. "I thought I recognized your bikes in the rack." He squeezed in line beside the boys, then made room for Curtis. "Thanks for saving our places."

"Yeah, thanks," mimicked Curtis, grinning.

"You pushed in!" the little girl behind them complained.

Wishbone eyed Curtis and Damont. "No cutting into the line."

Joe scowled. "No cutting in, guys."

"Didn't I just say that?" Wishbone sighed.

"The line moves fast," David said to Damont and Curtis. "But if I were you, I'd get to the end of it before it gets any longer."

Damont snorted and made a face. "I don't think so." He motioned with his head. "Come on, Curtis, let the master show you how it's done." He walked close to the head of the line. "Hey, don't I know you?" Damont said smoothly to a group of younger boys. He turned back to see if Joe and David were watching him make his move.

But the group of boys squeezed together so Damont and Curtis couldn't cut in line. Damont and Curtis tried their scam again at another spot, with the same results.

David shook his head. "Why don't they just get in the back of the line?"

Shrugging, Joe looked over his shoulder. "I don't know. But look how long the line is now."

Wishbone turned and looked over his tail. "Wow!"

Damont walked back to Joe and David. "See you, chumps. Thanks to you, we don't have time to eat. I have pressing business at the historical society."

"Yeah," said Curtis. "Damont's mom gave away some of his stuff, including his Bubba Bunny watch, from when he was a kid."

Damont glared at Curtis. "It *was* a cool watch when I was a kid. Something you wouldn't know about."

"And I need to get to the bike store and buy myself a new bicycle lock." Curtis smirked at Joe and David. "If you get my drift . . ."

David looked confused as Damont and Curtis walked away. "What do you think he meant by that?" he asked Joe.

Joe raised his eyebrows. "I have no idea."

As more people finished eating and squeezed out the door, the buffet line moved forward. Finally, it was Joe and David's turn to go inside and stand in front of the pizza pans and select their slices.

"Remember to get me a slice with pepperoni," Wishbone said, dancing around by Joe's feet so he wouldn't get stepped on.

David filled his plate first, then found them a booth. A few moments later, Joe slid in across from him.

"Now, *this* is what I call a great lunch," Wishbone said, sitting on the floor and gnawing on the pizza piece Joe handed him. "Okay. Now I'm ready for seconds."

In a while the boys stood, went and got more pizza, and brought it back to the table. But they didn't offer any to Wishbone.

"Joe, old buddy, old pal—where's mine?" Wishbone put a paw on Joe's leg and stared up at his friend. "Please, please, please. Just one more piece?" He stood and put both front paws on Joe's leg.

"No, Wishbone." Joe gently pushed him down.

"I wonder if any of these other nice people are skilled in the art of sharing." Wishbone edged toward a table with one adult and lots of children.

Joe checked his watch and stood up. "I have to get going. I promised my mom I'd clean out the garage."

David, Joe, and Wishbone squeezed past the people still waiting in line for pizza and stepped outside.

"I'm stuffed," Joe said. "I ate enough pizza to last me a week."

David put a hand on his stomach. "Me, too. It's too bad Sam is out of town."

Joe nodded.

Wishbone trotted ahead. He wondered exactly when Samantha Kepler—Joe and David's other close friend—would be back.

When Joe reached the bike rack, he tugged his bike backward. David's bike moved, too. Joe looked surprised. "I guess the pedals are tangled up together, or something."

Wishbone stepped closer as Joe bent down to get a better look. "Uh . . . Joe? You might want to look at the front tires."

Joe groaned as he discovered the problem. "I don't believe it!" He fingered an extra-long, old, rusty bicycle cable that had been hooked around the front tire of his bike, then wound through David's front tire. "I'd recognize this rusty cable anywhere," he said, holding it out for David to see. "It's Curtis's. Well, now we know what he meant by needing to get to the bike shop for a new lock."

13

He looked up, irritated. "This makes me angry. But I guess we're lucky he didn't lock our bikes to the rack, only to each other."

David dug into his pocket and pulled out some change. "I'll call my dad to come and get us." He went back inside, then came out a few minutes later. "The line is busy. It might be awhile."

"I'll try my mom." Joe left, then returned shortly, shaking his head. "She's not home. I got the machine."

David shrugged. "We'll just have to hold our front wheels off the ground and walk side by side."

"That's easier said than done." Joe grunted and groaned as he and David half-carried, half-wheeled their bikes toward home. A big rock lay in their path. Joe kicked it angrily. "Curtis is getting more like Damont every day." Panting, he changed his grip on the handlebar. The boys then turned onto another street.

Having their bikes locked together is going to make it a long trip home for Joe and David. It reminds me of the book *Kidnapped*, written by Robert Louis Stevenson, and published in 1886. In the story, David Balfour, a recently orphaned lad, sets out alone in 1751, across the Lowlands of Scotland. He plans to find an uncle he's never met and claim an inheritance that is owed to him. Does all go well for him on his travels? No, it does not. In fact, a lot goes wrong! Just thinking about David Balfour's adventures makes my fur stand on end. . . .

Chapter Two

Wishbone imagined himself as seventeen-year-old David Balfour, a lad born and raised in the Scottish Lowlands. The year was 1751, and Scotland was in a state of political unrest. A feud was taking place between the Lowlanders—the people who lived in the southern region of Scotland—and the Highlanders—the people who lived in the northern mountain region.

The Lowlanders supported King George II, who was from a German royal family, and ruled all of Great Britain, including Scotland. The Highlanders wanted to make a Scotsman named Prince Charles the ruler of Scotland and all of Great Britain. Because they wanted the current king out, the Highlanders were taking on England, as well as the Lowlanders.

In the middle of all this violence, Wishbone saw himself as the young David, telling his own story.

I could feel the early morning June sun on my furred back, and hear the blackbirds chirping in the garden

15

lilacs. I watched the mist that hung over the valley at dawn rise and then disappear as the air warmed up.

Using my teeth, I removed the key for the last time from the door of my father's house. It was a strange feeling, so odd that a shiver swept from my nose to my tail. The village of Essendean had been a good place to live, but there was nothing to keep me here any longer—I was now an orphan. My mother had died years ago, and my father more recently. I turned tail and walked away from the house, giving the ferns a last good sniff before I trotted on. The grass, which I had last rolled in the afternoon before, was still damp with dew and cold on my paws.

Waiting for me by the garden gate was Mr. Campbell, the minister of Essendean. He had been a very close friend to my father. Bending down, he clapped me on the back, ruffling my fur.

"Well, Davie, lad," said he, "I will go with ye as far as the ford, to set ye on the way."

A ford is a narrow part of a river or other body of water that can be crossed by walking. No dogpaddling necessary!

We began to walk forward in silence.

"Are ye sorry to leave Essendean?" he asked after a while.

My tail wagged slowly. "Sir, if I knew where I was going, and what would become of me, I would feel better. I'd cheerfully go anywhere if I thought I had a chance to better myself."

"Aye," said Mr. Campbell, nodding his agreement. "Very well, Davie. Then it is fitting for me to tell ye yer fortune." He gave me a kindly look. "Long after yer mother was gone, and yer father was near his end, he gave me a letter. He said it spoke of yer inheritance. Yer father said to me, 'When I am gone, and the house is in order, give my boy this letter and start him off to the house of Shaws. That is the place I came from, and where my boy should return.'"

"The house of Shaws!" I barked out in surprise. "But my father was poor. What had he to do with the house of Shaws?"

At that time, the word *house* didn't mean a place with three bedrooms, two bathrooms, and a big food bowl for the dog. *House* referred to the many generations of a noble family, all of whom had lived on the same large spread of land.

Relief swept over me as I realized I was not alone in the world—I had a family!

"Who can tell for sure?" Mr. Campbell said. "But the name of that family, Davie, my boy, is the name ye bear— Balfour of Shaws. It is an ancient, honest, very highly respected house."

We stopped at the edge of the ford. Mr. Campbell held the folded letter just inches from my black nose. I read aloud the words written in my father's own handwriting: "To Ebenezer Balfour, Esquire, of Shaws, in his house of Shaws, this will be delivered by my son, David Balfour." My heart beat hard and fast against my furry chest. I, the son of a poor country schoolmaster, had a rich family. Perhaps they served T-bones for breakfast, lunch, and dinner! I took the letter with my teeth. As I slipped it into my pocket, I took care not to disturb the wax seal holding the paper closed.

"Ye should get to the capital city of Edinburgh in two days of walking," said Mr. Campbell. "The house is near there, in Cramond." He put his arms around me and hugged me tightly. Then, stepping back, he held me at arm's length and looked at me with sadness in his eyes.

"If things do not go well for ye, ye are always welcome in my home, Davie."

Turning around quickly, and crying good-bye, Mr. Campbell set off, running in the direction from which we had come. I watched him hurry out of sight. I was going to miss Mr. Campbell. But I was happy to be leaving the quiet countryside to go north to a great, busy family—the house of Shaws. I would live among rich and respected gentlefolk of my own name and blood!

"Yes!" I flipped in the air, then walked into the ford. The water chilled my paws and legs. I walked tall to keep my underbelly dry.

When I reached the other side, I shook off any clinging water, then trotted on. So many rocks! So few trees! It made for a long, boring journey. All the while I kept wondering how I was related to Ebenezer Balfour. And why had my father—or my mother, for that matter—never spoken of him? I scratched my spotted ear as I wondered.

Just before noon of the second day I came to the top of a hill. I sat on my haunches and took a load off my hind paws. Looking over the edge of the hill, I saw the sea. Wow! Living all my life inland, I'd never seen anything so big and so wet. In an inlet, ships of different sizes lay anchored in the gently rolling water.

An inlet is a narrow strip of water running from a larger body of water into the land.

Halfway between me and the sea stood the bustling city of Edinburgh, full of smokestacks, which belched out big gray puffs from the factories. The turrets and walls of the city's castle, huge and brown, poked into the sky.

Raising my nose high, I breathed deeply, hoping to fill my lungs with a good dose of the salty sea air. *"Yuck!"*

I coughed and pawed my snout. What I got was smoke from the city's chimneys.

I continued my journey. At a shepherd's house, I stopped to ask directions to Cramond. Once there, I asked people about the Shaws. They looked at me strangely. At first I thought it was because of my appearance. My country clothing and the dust from the road that settled on them probably made the people think I wasn't of noble blood. But after three townsfolk had given me the same odd look and the same answer, I began to think there was something strange about the family of Shaws, not my looks.

I decided to change my tactics. Seeing an honest-looking fellow coming along a lane with his cart, I wagged my tail. "Have ye ever heard of the house of Shaws?" I asked.

He stopped and looked at me the same way the others had.

"Aye," said he, nodding. "Why?"

"Is it a *great* house?" I asked him, perking up my ears hopefully.

Said he, "The house is a big house."

"I don't mean the size of the house. What I mean," said I, "is what about the folk who live there?"

"Folk?" cried he, screwing up his face. "Are ye crazy? There's no folk there."

My tail stopped wagging, but my heart pounded furiously. "Not Mr. Ebenezer?"

"Aye," said the man. "There's the owner, if it's him ye're wanting." The man raised his eyebrows and continued. "Ye seem a decent lad, and if ye'll take a word from me, ye'll keep clear of the Shaws." Abruptly, he hurried off.

Helllooo! I cannot describe the feelings that shot through me! My dreams were shattered. I wanted to let out a great howl, but held it inside for fear that people nearby would think me insane. Should I turn tail and go home? No, I'd come too far to do that. I needed to see where the Shaws lived, and Ebenezer, with my own eyes.

I scratched a flea, then pushed on. Near sundown I met a heavyset, sour-looking woman trudging down a hill. I held up a paw and waved to her. "Could ye point me in the direction of the Shaws?" I asked.

Turning around without speaking a word, the woman walked with me back up the hill she'd just left. She pointed to a big, gloomy-looking building standing alone at the bottom of the next valley. The countryside around it was pleasant—low hills with plenty of bushes to sniff. And the crops looked wonderfully good, perfect for running through and munching on. But the building itself appeared to be in ruin. No road led up to it, and no smoke rose from any of its chimneys.

"That?" I barked in surprise. "That is where all the branches of my family have lived for so many years?"

The woman's face lit up with anger. "That is it!" she cried. "Blood built it. Blood stopped the building of it. Blood shall bring it down!" She spat. "If ye see the man who lives there, tell him Jennet Clouston has again called down the curse on him!" She turned and fled.

"Whoa!" My legs suddenly felt weak. I sat down in a ditch and stared at the building. I cocked my head. The more I looked around, the more pleasant the countryside appeared. The hawthorn bushes were full of white and pink flowers, and the fields were dotted with sheep. A flock of blackbirds flew across the sky. All of these were signs of good living. But the run-down building in the midst of the beauty made me shiver and my fur bristle.

Now, what? I wondered, lying down and resting my head on my paws. At last the sun went down. That was when I saw smoke scrolling from the chimney into the sky. It was a thin stream, like smoke wafting from a candle, but it was definitely smoke. And it meant there was a fire, which meant warmth and food, and a living person inside. I stood, a small ray of hope burning in me.

"Ready or not, here I come."

Putting my nose to the ground, I sniffed until I found a faint trail in the grass. I followed it toward the house and came upon two stone pillars, which were not connected to anything. Plainly, I could see this was meant to be the main entrance, but it had never been finished. Weeds scratched my underbelly as I inched on toward the house.

What a dreary sight that house was! I squinted into the dusk for a clearer view. One wing had never been completed. It stood open to the elements on the upper floors, and showed against the sky with unfinished steps and stairs. Many of the windows were broken. Bats flew in and out of the unfinished wing like black ghosts. Was this really the great estate I'd been searching for? It didn't look fit for man or beast.

Paw by paw I inched my way closer. The shimmering light of a small fire began to glimmer as I saw through the lower windows. My keen ears picked up the sound of rattling dishes, then coughing. I finally got close enough to lift my paw and scratch on the nail-studded door. "Hello? . . . Anybody home?"

The house fell silent. Then, suddenly, I heard coughing directly above me. Smelling danger, I jumped back and looked up. A man's head in a nightcap, and the end of a big gun, poked out from one of the windows.

"It's loaded," warned a voice. "What do ye want?"

"I have come with a letter for Mr. Ebenezer Balfour of Shaws," I said. "Is he here?"

22

"Ye can put it down upon the doorstep, and then be off with ye," the voice replied.

"I will do no such thing." I sat down firmly on my haunches.

"Who are ye?" he asked.

"David Balfour."

At that remark, the man seemed startled, and the gun rattled on the windowsill. With a curious change of voice, the man asked, "Is yer father dead?"

I was too stunned to speak.

"Aye," the man said, "he's dead, no doubt, and that's what brings ye to my door. I'll let ye in." His hand disappeared from the window. Soon I heard a great rattling of chains and bolts. The door opened slowly.

I stared into the darkness beyond, trying to see my surroundings.

"Go toward the firelight, into the kitchen, and be sure to touch nothing," said the voice.

As I sniffed my way toward the kitchen firelight, I heard the man put the chains and bolts back in place. Except for a few dishes and a few locked chests, the kitchen was empty. I sniffed the floor for crumbs. None. And the place smelled moldy and damp!

The man joined me shortly. He was a stooped, clay-faced creature with a mean look and an untidy beard. He could have been anywhere between fifty and seventy. But it was the way he kept watching me, yet wouldn't look me directly in the eye, that made me feel most uncomfortable.

He gave me a bowl of cold porridge. I tried not to make a face as I lapped up the awful-tasting mush. No bones about it—I was starved! Unlocking a chest, the man poured himself some ale. "Now give me Alexander's letter."

Shocked, I let out a yip. "Ye know my father's name?"

"It would be strange if I didn't, for he was my born brother. And little as ye seem to like me or my house or my good porridge, I'm yer born uncle, Davie, my man. And ye are my born nephew."

The news hit me like a ton of bricks. "Why haven't I heard of ye until now?" I took the letter from my pocket and gave it to him.

"It matters none. The past is past." The stranger—my uncle—stooping closer to the fire, turned the letter over and over in his hands. He looked at me slyly. "Do ye know what's in here?"

I shook my head, flipping an ear back in the process. "No, sir. Ye can see for yerself the seal is unbroken."

He broke the seal and read the letter, then refolded it. "And what are yer hopes, Davie, my man?"

"I confess, sir, when I was told I had a well-to-do family, I began to hope that they might help me in my life. But I am no beggar. I look for no special favors, only the true inheritance that is meant to be mine."

He continued to throw out little darting glances. Once our eyes met. My uncle looked worried, like a thief caught with his hand in someone's pocket.

Finally he came very close to me and hit me right upon my furred shoulder. "I'm glad I let ye in. But hoots-toots, I'm not a warlock. I can't find a fortune at the bottom of a porridge bowl. Give me a few days and I'll get ye yer money." He half-smiled. "And now, Davie, my man, come to yer bed."

To my surprise, my uncle lit no lantern or candle. We groped our way down a dark passage and up a flight of steps. Stopping at a door, he unlocked it. Then he motioned me in.

24

"Could I have a light?" I asked, stepping inside. The room was as cold as a well. A shiver ran from my nose to my tail. "It's as black as tar in here."

"Hoot-toot!" said Uncle Ebenezer with disapproval. "There's a fine moon tonight." He yanked the door shut. Then I heard him lock me in from the outside.

"Hey—this is not at all what I had in mind!" I growled, giving the door a couple of frustrated scratches with one of my paws.

I continued to shiver as I finally lay down and curled up. I slept through the night on a bed as damp as what might be found in a dungeon.

At the first light of day I awoke. My room was huge, and at one time it must have been quite pleasant. But over the years, dampness, dirt, mice, and spiders had done their worst damage.

I scratched at the door until my uncle came and let me out. He led me to the kitchen and gave me porridge. "What's mine is yers, Davie, my man. Blood is thicker than water, and we are the last of the Balfours." His eyes, however, with their darting glances, told me differently.

Still, I listened as he rambled on about the family and its centuries-old greatness. He told me how his father— the grandfather I had never known—had begun to enlarge the house, and how he, himself, had stopped the building because he felt it was a waste. This reminded me of Jennet Clouston's message. I cocked my head and repeated her words to my uncle.

"That woman has cursed me one too many times!" he cried. "I'll be off this instant to have her proclaimed a witch!" He opened a chest and got out a very old, blue vest, and a beaver hat, both without lace.

No, not ruffly lace! "Lace" is what people called the ornamental braid used to trim coats and uniforms.

"I cannot leave ye by yerself in the house," said my uncle, struggling into the coat. "I'll have to lock ye out."

The blood rushed to my face. My whiskers pricked up. Was he just looking for a way to get me out of there? "If ye lock me out," I growled, "it'll be the last ye see of me in friendship."

Twitching and trembling, Uncle Ebenezer went and looked out a window for a while. "I'll not go, then."

"Uncle Ebenezer," said I, "ye treat me like a thief. If ye don't like me, why are ye going to help me?"

"I like ye fine, Davie, my man," he said earnestly. "Stay for a while and ye'll find that we agree on things."

I thought about the matter silently, then slowly wagged my tail. "Okay. It's better I should be helped by my own family than by my friend, the minister Mr. Campbell."

The strange smile that spread across my uncle's face made me wonder if I had made the right decision.

Chapter Three

I spent the next few days reading books in a room next to the kitchen. I was almost enjoying myself. But the sight of my uncle—his eyes playing hide-and-seek with mine—always kept me watchful.

In this same room I also dug up something that confused me. Printed neatly inside the cover of one book was this inscription: TO EBENEZER ON HIS FIFTH BIRTHDAY—LOVE, ALEXANDER. I touched the writing with my paw. If Ebenezer was only five, and my father was the younger brother, how could he write this? It was fine penmanship. Was my father actually the older one? But if that was so, the house of Shaws would have belonged to my father, not to Ebenezer. The older son always inherited everything. The younger ones didn't get so much as a dried-up bone! At supper I questioned my uncle.

He jumped up from his stool, spilling his porridge, and grabbed me by the front of my jacket. "Why do ye ask that?"

I let out a low growl. "Take yer hand off me!"

My uncle obeyed, as if he'd been to obedience school. Then he went back to his stool. "Ye should not speak to me about my brother," he said, with more coldness in his voice than a frosty wind.

I began to wonder if my uncle was insane.

Then he did the strangest thing. He got up, went over to one of the chests, and unlocked it. Then he opened it just enough to slip his hand inside and pull out some money. He counted out thirty golden pieces for me. "This is separate from yer inheritance," Ebenezer said. "It's money I promised ye before ye were born. That'll show ye. I'm an odd man, but my word is my pledge, and this is the proof of it. Now I think we'll agree as friends should." He placed the coins on the table, in front of me.

I don't think so, I thought silently. But aloud, I thanked him. Using my teeth, I took all the coins and dropped them into the money purse hanging from my neck.

"Tit for tat," said he, looking at me sideways. "Now ye must prove yer gratitude. I'm growing old and would like yer help with the repair of the house and replanting the garden."

I wagged my tail to show my readiness to serve. I was sure that my gardening and digging abilities would pleasantly surprise him.

Uncle Ebenezer pulled a rusty key from his pocket. "Here's the key to the tower door at the far end of the house. Ye can get to the tower only from the outside, for that part of the house is not finished. Go up the stairs and bring me down the chest that's at the top."

I took the key in my teeth, waited for him to unbolt the door, then stepped into the darkness. "Can I have a lantern?" I mumbled.

"No lanterns in my house," he said slyly.

Ye have got to be kidding, I thought. "I hope the stairs are in good repair."

"They're solid," said he. As I left, he added, "But keep to the wall. There's no handrail."

The wind moaned in the distance as I made my way through the black night. I had just stuck my key into the tower door when lightning lit up the sky, half-blinding me. The fur on my neck bristled.

I stepped into the tower. It was so dark inside I couldn't see my paw in front of my black nose. Feeling my way along the wall, I made my way up the steep, spiraling stone staircase. The narrow steps were icy-cold against my paws. My heart pounded. With each step I climbed, the stair-tower grew windier.

"What's going on?" I wondered. Then another blink of summer lightning brightened the sky. Fear gripped me by the throat like a choker chain. The flash had shown me that I was climbing open framework, and that the steps were of unequal length. What really sent a shiver down my spine was the fact that one of my paws rested on the very edge of a steep step. One wrong move and I'd be free-falling down the shaft in the center of the stairwell!

This is not a finished staircase! I thought. *It's a deathtrap.* There was no chest. My uncle was trying to kill me!

Bats flew at me from the top of the tower. I shook my head and barked loudly to keep them away, being careful not to make a move that would throw me off balance and send me over the side. Dropping to my belly, I turned around. The cold from the stone steps seeped through my fur as I felt my way downward, paw by paw. Halfway down, one front paw slipped upon an outer edge of a step and found nothing but air beyond. I shivered and let out a howl. Soon, wind shook the tower and rain started to fall. Before I reached ground level the rain fell in buckets. Thunder boomed and lightning flashed.

My fur was soaked and my paws were muddy by the time I reached the door to the house. I shook. Then I pushed on the door, which had been left ajar. I crept silently inside and toward the kitchen. My uncle, his back toward me at the table, shuddered and groaned aloud.

I sneaked up behind him, then jumped up and clapped my paws on the back of his chair. "Aha!" I barked.

My uncle cried out, flung his arms in the air, then tumbled to the floor like a dead man.

As I sucked in my breath, he peeked at me with one eye. At that moment I knew he was only pretending to play dead.

I nosed his foot. "Sit up!" I cried.

"Are ye alive?" he sobbed. "Oh, Davie, are ye alive?"

"Yes," said I. "No thanks to ye!"

My uncle looked small and pale, sitting on the floor. He patted his chest. "I have a little heart trouble, Davie."

I sat down firmly on my haunches and stared at him. I wanted some answers. "Why do ye lock me in at night? Why do ye lie about being friends? And why did ye just now try to kill me?"

He listened in silence. Then, in a broken voice, he begged me to let him go to bed.

"I'll tell ye in the morning," he said. "As sure as death, I will."

He was so weak, I agreed. I even helped him up the stairs. Afterward, I didn't go on to my room. Instead, I returned to the kitchen, built up the fire, and lay down. Soon I was dry and warm from nose to tail. But my sleep was fitful as I listened for my uncle to stir. There was no doubt that I held my life in my own four paws.

The next morning Uncle Ebenezer appeared in the kitchen and acted as if nothing had happened.

"Have ye nothing more to say?" I cried. When he made no attempt to reply, I went on. "What causes ye to cheat me, and to attempt to—"

He waved his hand. "It was all in jest, Davie, my man. I like a bit of fun." He shuffled over to the table and sat down.

"Jest? Fun? How could—"

I was interrupted by a knock at the door. I went over, unlatched it with my paw, and pulled it open. On the doorstep stood a half-grown boy in sea clothes. He looked cold.

"I've brought a letter from Captain Hoseason," he said as soon as the door was open. "I'm a cabin boy on his ship. The letter is for Mr. Balfour." He shivered. "And I say, mate, I'm so hungry I could die right here."

I stepped aside. "Come into the house. Ye shall have a bite, even if I have to give ye my own porridge."

I took him to the kitchen, where he greedily helped himself to the rest of my breakfast. Meanwhile, my uncle read the letter. Then he got to his feet with great liveliness. He pulled me into the farthest corner of the room.

"I have business with Hoseason, the captain of a trading ship, the *Covenant*. And as ye can read for yourself," Ebenezer said, pushing the letter toward me, "the wind is right and the ship will be leaving Queensferry today. The letter instructs me to meet him at the inn, where I must sign papers for the captain before he sails."

While keeping his eyes on the boy, Ebenezer leaned a little closer to my spotted ear and lowered his voice.

"Now, if ye and I were to walk with the lad back to the inn where the captain is staying, I could get my business taken care of. Then, so our trip wouldn't be a waste, we could go to see my lawyer, Mr. Rankeillor. Ye may not believe me, but Rankeillor's a respected man, and he liked yer father. He'll show ye, Davie, that I have always had only yer best interests at heart."

I couldn't help but notice his darting glances as I considered his invitation. These places my uncle had just spoken of would be full of people—he couldn't attempt any violence toward me there. The presence of the cabin boy would serve as added protection. And it would be wonderful to have a close-up view of the sea! I wagged my tail. "Very well."

Quickly my uncle got into his hat and coat, then put on an old rusty sword. He locked the door behind us and we set forth.

It was June, and the grass was white with daisies, but the wind blew cold, as if it were a frosty winter's day. Uncle Ebenezer hurried along, leaving me to walk with the cabin boy. I found out his name was Ransome, and that he'd been going out to sea since he was nine. He'd lost track of time, though, and couldn't tell me exactly how old he was.

"The *Covenant* is the finest ship that's ever sailed." Ransome smiled. "And Captain Hoseason is rough, fierce, and as thieving as they come!" he said proudly.

You could have knocked me over with a kitten's whisker. This poor cabin boy was admiring these brutal qualities!

"But he's not a good seaman," Ransome said, shaking his head. "It's the first mate, Mr. Shuan, who navigates the ship. He's the finest seaman in the trade, except when he drinks." Pulling down his stocking, he showed me a raw, red wound that made my blood run cold. "Mr. Shuan did that."

"Why do ye let him do that to ye?"

33

Ransome smiled and then pulled back his shirt to expose a great knife. "Someday he'll get exactly what he deserves."

I shuddered as I stared at the knife.

Coming over a hill, the three of us stopped and looked down upon the water. Ransome pointed in the distance offshore. "The *Covenant*. She's too big a ship to come any closer." Next, he pointed to a small rowboat tied to a high dock at the water's edge. "That skiff will take us to her."

"Well, what are we standing here for?" my uncle asked. "It's icy cold, and if I'm not mistaken, the crew is readying the *Covenant* to go to sea. Hoseason will be leaving soon."

As I trotted beside them heading down the hill toward the stone inn, I raised my nose high up and sniffed deep breaths of the salty air. There was an energizing freshness about it—a nice change from the stale, musty smell in Ebenezer's dingy house.

As we walked onto the beach, I stopped to taste some clusters of green and brown weeds. Trotting over to the shore, I barked and jumped and chased the waves, then jumped out of their way when they rolled toward me. Finally, I ran to catch up with my companions. Ransome went to the rowboat, while Uncle Ebenezer and I headed to the inn.

Inside, my uncle stopped me. "Ye wait by the fire while I attend to business."

That suited me fine. I shook the cold off my fur, then curled up close to the fire. The kindly looking innkeeper smiled at me. I smiled back, and I thought I'd take advantage of his friendliness. "Do ye know the lawyer Mr. Rankeillor?"

"Hoot, yes," said he, tidying up the room. "A very

honest man." He paused. "And are ye a friend of Ebenezer's?"

I saw the look of dismay on the innkeeper's face. "No." I shook my head.

"He's a wicked old man," said the innkeeper, dusting a lamp. "There's many who would like to see him hanging in the wind. And yet he was a fine young fellow once." He shook his head. "But that was before word got around that he killed Mr. Alexander."

I bolted up to all fours. People here thought Ebenezer had killed my father! "And why would Ebenezer kill him?" I asked.

"For the place. Alexander was the older. The Shaws belonged to him," said the innkeeper, leaving the room.

I dropped to my haunches, stunned. If it was true that my father was the elder, then everything was rightfully mine, not Ebenezer's. I was rich, rich, rich! So why had my father left his home?

The next thing I heard was the voice of my uncle calling to me, so I trotted over. He introduced me to the *Covenant*'s captain, who kept praising my looks. It was great having someone finally notice my unique and superb markings!

"Time is too short to strike up much of a close friendship," the captain said to me. "But we'll try with the little time we have." He smiled. "Please do me the honor of walking me to the rowboat."

That was how I liked to be treated—with respect! I wagged my tail and held my head high as we left the inn. I walked with the captain and my uncle. The captain stayed at my side and asked me questions about my life on land. He made me feel as important as a king! In no time we were at the dock, walking across the wooden planks, some of which had rotting spots just the right size to catch a paw and twist a leg.

"Would both of ye like a tour of the *Covenant?*" asked the captain. "It's an offer I don't make to every man."

I really wanted to see that ship up close! But I didn't trust my uncle and didn't want to put myself in danger. My safety seemed guaranteed as long as we were in the safe sight of others. "We have an appointment with the lawyer," I said.

Hoseason nodded. "Aye, aye. That's what yer uncle said. But after ye have seen the *Covenant,* the rowboat can put ye ashore near Rankeillor's house." Then he suddenly leaned down and whispered in my brown ear, "Take care of yer uncle. The old fox means mischief. Come aboard so we can talk."

The captain's generosity got the better of me, and I must admit I was as curious as a new pup. Ransome had rejoined our group, and he lowered me into the wooden rowboat as my uncle and Captain Hoseason climbed aboard. Boy, was I surprised by the other four scary-looking seamen already on the boat. As I stared at the men, the oars sliced through the water and the rowboat lurched toward the big ship. The men were large fellows. While I was jerked off balance by the boat's movements, they didn't budge a bit.

Maybe they were weighted down by their weapons. One man had pistols stuck in all of his pockets. Another had knotty clubs in his belt. And the other two had knives in sheaths strapped around their waists. I also noticed some wore colored handkerchiefs tied around their throats.

"Hi, guys. Nice collars." I wagged my tail at the men, but they looked about as friendly as a pack of wild

beasts! The one nearest me kept grumbling and groaning that this harbor didn't have enough taverns. I was relieved when, fifteen minutes later, we pulled up safely alongside the *Covenant*.

The ship was huge. Not only was it long from end to end, but two poles that supported sails rose high into the sky. Later, I found out these poles were called masts. Except for a castle, this ship was the biggest thing that I'd ever seen.

Captain Hoseason patted my shoulder and declared that he and I must be the first to board the *Covenant*. I was impressed by how he treated me like his equal!

A small, square, wooden platform was lowered by ropes from the ship. Captain Hoseason stepped onto it and was hoisted into the air by equipment on the ship. When he was safely on board, the platform was then sent down for me.

There were no sides to the platform. I took a deep breath, then nervously climbed onto it one paw at a time. "No safety net, huh?" Suddenly I was hoisted and tossed into the air. It felt as if my stomach had been left in the rowboat. The next thing I knew, I was being put down roughly on the deck of the ship. I swaggered off the platform, dizzy and unsteady, and stood next to the captain's feet. I watched the sailors work and talk as they brought another sailor up. Finally my sea legs took hold—all four at once—and I was fine.

Wow! So many strange sights and smells! The captain began to point out parts of the ship and tell me their names and uses. He nodded to a long pole sticking out from the front of the ship. "That's the bowsprit. As ye can see, it supports the sail rigging." He made a sweeping gesture with his hand, pointing from one end of the ship to the other. "She's glorious from stem to stern. The stem is forward, and the stern is the rear of the ship."

Suddenly I sensed something had changed. My eyes darted from side to side. "Where is my uncle?"

"Aye," said Hoseason grimly, "that's the point."

"What do ye mean, 'that's the point'?"

The captain was silent, and I knew I was in trouble.

Something was very wrong! With all of my strength, I ran to the edge of the ship. I jumped up on a keg, put my front paws on the railing, and looked over it. Sure enough, there was the rowboat going toward town, with my uncle sitting at the tail end. I cried out—"Help! Help!" I had left my father's house only a week ago, and already I was in a pack of trouble.

Strong hands tugged on my fur and tried to yank me back from the railing. My uncle turned around in his seat and shot me a smile so cruel and wicked that it filled me with terror. Every inch of my fur bristled.

That smile was the last thing I saw for a while. A thunderbolt seemed to strike me with a great flash of fire. Then I fell to the deck, unconscious.

Wow! This sounds like the adventure of a life-time: a country lad, a dishonest captain, and a desperate-looking crew, all aboard the same ship! What more could anyone ask for? Hmmm . . . How about a life raft?

Maybe I had better see how Joe and David are getting along with their bikes.

Chapter Four

Joe and David made it back to the Barneses' garage. They held their bikes steady while Mr. Barnes used his hacksaw to cut the rusty cable that connected them.

"That was a pretty mean trick Curtis pulled," he said, as he finished and put the saw away.

The boys looked at each other.

"You're telling us!" David wheeled his bike to the corner.

"He's a real pain," Joe said. "Thanks for the help, Mr. Barnes." Joe rolled his bike outside. "I need to clean out the garage before we look for a campsite, David. I'll see you later."

"Okay. 'Bye." David waved.

"Race you home!" Wishbone tore across the cul-de-sac and onto the Talbots' front porch. "And the winner is the cute terrier with the spotted ear!" He scratched at the door. "Ellen? You in there?"

Joe put his bike in the garage, then went and opened the back door to the house.

"Excuse me, hungry dog coming through. Snack

time!" Wishbone charged inside and ran to the ginger-snap cabinet.

"Mom?" Joe called. "I'm home." He went into the kitchen, turned on the faucet at the sink, and ran himself a full glass of water. He drank half of it, then noticed a note on the kitchen table. Plopping into a chair, he read it:

Dear Joe,
I decided to stop off at the library on my way to the store. I should be home between 3:30 and 4:00.
Mom

Joe checked his watch. "I'd better get started on the garage."

Still standing at the cabinet, Wishbone stared at Joe. "How about a snack?" Wishbone sighed. "There has to be a reason why he doesn't listen to me. Maybe it has to do with the shape of his ears—they are awfully small. Oh, well . . ." After taking a quick drink from his bowl, he trotted outside after Joe.

When Joe pulled open the garage door, Wishbone stepped inside. He sniffed his way across the smooth, cool floor while Joe brushed the cobwebs off a lawn chair and set it up in the driveway. Immediately, Wishbone backtracked and jumped up into it.

"I'll supervise the clean-up. So far, you're doing fine." Lying down, he rested his head on his paws and watched Joe bring more items out of the garage and sort them into two piles—one to keep, one to give away.

When he came to his sleeping bag, Joe took it and set it down by itself on the lawn. Then he held up a bright orange cloth and smiled. "Hey, here's the pup tent!"

Looks more like an oversized raincoat to me, Wishbone thought.

41

Joe sat down by Wishbone and began to open up the tent. He held the top up to a point. "Home, sweet home."

"Uh . . . where's the kitchen?" Wishbone asked. "You don't expect me to stay someplace without a kitchen, do you?"

Joe fiddled with the tent for a while, then finally rolled it up and set it down over by his sleeping bag. He sorted through more of his stuff. Wishbone watched as the piles in the driveway got bigger and bigger.

"My flashlight!"

Wishbone perked up. "You make it sound better than finding a squeaky toy."

Joe turned it on to see if the batteries were still good. "Great!" He smiled, turned the light off, and looked over his shoulder at the tent. Then he checked his watch. "Almost three o'clock. Mom won't be back for at least another half hour. Come on, Wishbone!" he said excitedly. "Let's go get David. If we hurry, we can still pick out a campsite and return to clean up before mom returns."

Wishbone bolted to his feet, then stopped and looked around. "Uh . . . Joe? There's stuff all over the driveway." He watched as Joe jogged across the yard. "Okay. It'll wait." Jumping down from the chair, Wishbone scampered after Joe.

He caught up with him on David's front porch and waited while Joe rang the bell.

When the door opened, Wishbone took a step back. "Emily! Only a kindergartner, but big enough to cause a lot of trouble."

"Wishbone!" David's little sister, Emily, bent down and smothered him with a hug.

Sighing, Wishbone tried to back away. "Have you

ever heard of the expression 'If you love something, let it go'?"

David popped into the doorway. "Hi, Joe." He looked down. "Emily, let go of Wishbone."

"Thank you, David."

Emily released Wishbone and he stepped over to the side, so Joe stood between him and Emily.

"David, do you want to look for a campsite now?" Joe asked.

David made a face. "Can't. I promised Emily I'd show her some games on the computer."

"Too bad," Joe said, and glanced longingly in the general direction of Jackson Park.

Emily giggled and took a step toward Wishbone.

"Sorry." David shrugged. "We could wait to look for a site tomorrow . . ."

"David seems to have noticed the same eager look on your face that I see," Wishbone said to Joe.

"Or you and Wishbone could do it now." David smiled.

Wishbone kept his eyes on Emily, taking a step back for each one she took toward him. "That's a terrific idea, David." He lowered his voice. "Let's get out of here, Joe, before this tiger with a cute smile springs at me again.

Joe nodded. "That'd be great. I'm really looking forward to tomorrow night!" Joe turned and walked off the front porch, with Wishbone at his side.

"'Bye, Wishbone," Emily called after them. "See you later."

"Thanks for the warning, Emily."

Wishbone trotted ahead of Joe, sniffing out the trail leading into the park.

"Trees—trees everywhere! Yahoo!" Wishbone flipped in the air, then ran in a circle. "I love Jackson Park!" When the trail forked, he stopped and waited for Joe. "This way!" Wishbone darted to the left. But Joe took the right fork, and Wishbone had to cut through some scratchy brush to catch up with him. "You should've listened to me, Joe."

Stopping, Joe eyed a flat, grassy area.

"Too close to the trail."

He walked over to a nearby shady area.

"This is nice and flat."

He looked toward the sky, then back and forth between the treetops.

"I don't know. Too many trees."

"Oh!" Wishbone gasped. "You didn't say too many trees, did you, Joe? There can never be too many trees!"

Joe headed off with quick steps. "Let's keep looking. There's bound to be lots of good camping spots in this big park."

Wishbone bounded after him. They stopped at two maybes. Wishbone sniffed each site. "These are both good choices, Joe." As he waited for Joe to make a decision, he rolled in the grass, rubbing its good earthy smell across every inch of his body. "This and a 'no-cat zone' are my idea of heaven."

Joe took off up the trail.

Wishbone sneezed the grass from his nose and tore off after him. "Uhhh! We aren't going to sleep in the baseball field, are we? There aren't any trees there."

As soon as Joe changed direction again, Wishbone relaxed. He knew exactly where Joe was headed. It was part of the park that was very special to Joe, because Joe had gone there with his father many times before his father died.

"Going to the tire swing, right?" Suddenly, Wishbone stopped and pricked up his ears. "Wait, Joe, I hear something."

Joe kept walking. Then all at once he stopped, too, and listened. Leaning forward, he peeked through the bushes and trees.

Wishbone trotted quietly up beside him. Ahead of them, sitting on the tire swing with his back to them, was Curtis. He wrote something in a spiral notebook on his lap, then held it up to read, muttering. Then he put the notebook back in his lap and erased. Write, mutter, erase. Write, mutter, erase . . .

Joe whispered, "I wonder what he's doing there. Whatever he's writing, it sounds as if it's something important."

Wishbone cocked his head and listened.

Without looking away from his paper, Curtis reached down, pulled something from a bag on the ground, then shoved it into his mouth.

Wishbone wagged his tail. "Cookies! A whole bag, and it's got my name written all over it." Wishbone leaped from between the trees. "Snack time!" he barked.

Joe raced out with him.

Startled, Curtis jumped out of the swing so fast that his notebook flew out of his hands and fell onto the ground.

Immediately, Joe scooped up the notebook and glanced at the page. "It's a letter to your dad."

"Give me that!" Curtis grabbed at the paper, but Joe held it out of his reach.

"What's the big idea of locking my bike to David's at Pepper Pete's?" Joe asked.

45

"No big idea," Curtis said, standing tall. "It was your fault for not letting us cut in line." He took a step forward. "It was a joke. Now give me my notebook! It's personal."

Wishbone looked up while he chewed another cookie. "Mmm . . . good. You know, Curtis, from the way you're fidgeting, I'd say you're not so cocky when the Damonster isn't by your side." He sniffed. "My nose says he's nowhere near here."

"Yeah, well, I take what you did to David and me personally, too." Joe locked stares with Curtis, then finally thrust the notebook toward him.

Curtis took a step toward Joe and snatched the notebook. "It's personal. And you were spying on me!"

"No, I wasn't." Joe scowled. "I was just walking by."

Curtis hid the writing against his shirt. "Mind your own business, Talbot."

"And you mind yours." Joe turned to Wishbone. "Come on, Wishbone!" he said sternly.

Wishbone obediently went and sat by Joe's feet.

"Boy, is there tension here!" He looked up and saw that Joe had locked eyes with Curtis.

"Don't tell anybody," Curtis threatened. "You got it, Talbot?"

"No problem. I'm not the one who goes around and tries to embarrass people."

Curtis stared at him with a puzzled look on his face.

"Remember?" said Joe. "In Ms. Malloy's class, you grabbed the paper I was doodling on."

Curtis scowled.

"I remember," Wishbone said. "It was when you had a crush on your teacher. You made up a crossword puzzle using her name."

Joe bent down and scratched Wishbone between the ears. Then he stood and said, "Let's go, boy."

Wishbone spent the next ten minutes sniffing the bushes, while Joe searched out more possible camping sites.

Finally, Joe stopped, turned around, and walked back the way they'd come. "Let's go back. I think the best site is the one on the other side of the tire swing."

"But, Joe, I think I just spotted a squirrel. Joe?" Wishbone followed his pal. "Okay, I'm sure there are more where we're going."

Joe circled wide to pass the swing. As Wishbone peered through the tall grass, he saw Curtis still sitting in the tire, writing and erasing.

"Stay with me," Joe whispered to Wishbone. Not far beyond the swing, but out of range of Curtis's sight and hearing, Joe stopped. He paced off the ground. "Great! This is the perfect spot for the tent. Nice and flat. We'll get a lot of light from the moon, and we have a tree, too."

"Thank you." Wishbone pawed the air happily. "Best of all, I can see that lamppost . . . in case somebody gets scared. Not that I'd ever get scared. There's nothing to be frightened of around here at night." Wishbone stared into the shadows. "Hmm . . . Cats are nocturnal—they stalk at night. There aren't any *big* cats—like lions or tigers—around here. Nothing to fear, Joe."

Wishbone shivered at the thought.

"Two boys and one cute dog, all alone, facing dangers in the dark."

Then Wishbone thought of David Balfour, kidnapped from the shores of Scotland and sent to sea on a ship called the *Covenant*. David was all alone to face his enemies. How would he ever escape? Even if he did, where could he go? The sea surrounded him like a giant cage.

Wishbone's Sailing Dictionary for Persons Lost at Sea and Other Interested Parties

aye	yes
berth	a place to sit or sleep on a ship
bow	the front of the ship (pronounced like the *bow* in *bow-wow*)
bowsprit	a thick, strong pole that projects forward from the front of a ship and is used to support sail rigging
brig	ship
cutlass	a short, curved sword carried by sailors
first mate	an officer on a ship
forecastle	the forward part of the upper deck of a ship—it's where the crew is housed
head wind	a wind blowing in the opposite direction of where the ship is going. In dog-speak, that means it's a wind that blows directly at your face.
helm	a lever or wheel for steering the ship
hold	the area of the ship belowdecks where the cargo is kept
landlubber	someone who is unfamiliar with the sea or sailing

mast	a long pole that rises from the deck of a ship and supports the sails and rigging
port	the left side of the ship
reef	a chain of rocks near the surface of the water
rigging	the ropes that are used to raise and lower the sails, and move them to and fro
roundhouse	Whoever named this was really confused! This is the captain's quarters, and it's not round at all. The first and second mates live here, too. The roundhouse also contains the chart room, where the ship's progress is planned, and plotted on maps.
sea dog	an experienced sailor
second mate	the other officer on the ship
ship's stores	the ship's supplies, such as food and other items
skiff	a light rowboat
starboard	the right side of the ship
stem	the front of a ship, or forward
stern	the tail end of a ship, or rear
swell	gigantic wave
tiller	handle used to turn the rudder in steering a boat

Chapter Five

I awoke in total darkness, all four of my paws tied with rope. My head ached as if I'd run into a castle wall at full speed. The noises around me were deafening— roaring water, thrashing spray, the thundering of sails, and the shrill cries of the seamen. The room I was in heaved upward, then crashed down, leaving me dizzy. *Where am I?* I wondered.

I heard a bell, then loud footsteps above me. My eyes were useless in the blackness that surrounded me, so I put my nose to work. My first sniff told me a bowl of stew was nearby, and also rope and canvas. I realized I must be in the belly of the ship with the spare sails and rigging. The ship rose even higher than before, then crashed down again. The wind had apparently strengthened, and we were being tossed around like an old sock.

When I realized how bad my situation was, my head ached even more. I lost all hope. Had I been taken away from Scotland to be sold in another country to do forced labor? Would these men aboard ship kill me? I could have kicked myself for being tricked by my uncle and the captain! I would gladly have chewed their shoes into

Vivian Sathre

jerky for all their trickery! But the sorry fact was that I had become as helpless as a newborn pup.

I burrowed my nose into my front paws and began gnawing at the rope that held them tightly tied together. Being a landlubber and unused to the rolling sea, I suddenly felt ill. My stomach began its own rolling, different from the violent movements of the ship. The smell of my nearby pan of food made me feel like gagging. That was certainly a first!

Weak and woozy, I lay back. If only I had some fresh grass to nibble on—I'm sure that would have made me feel better. Finally, sleep took me away from my misery and sorrow.

From then on my senses came and went. I had no measure of time. Day and night were alike in the awful-smelling cavern where I lay. I became weaker and weaker.

I was suddenly awakened by the light of a hand lantern shining in my face. A small man with green eyes and a tangle of light hair stood looking down at me.

"Well," said he, "I'm Mr. Riach, second mate of this ship. How are ye?"

I whimpered. Then, using only my eyes, I looked around. I'd been right about being placed with the spare sails and rigging. There were also a few chests and kegs in this storeroom, perhaps full of supplies.

"Ye're in the hold with the cargo." He nodded at my food dish. "Ye haven't touched yer meat."

I forced my head up. "I can't bear to look at it," I whispered. Then I lay down again. I felt so hot that for the first time I wished my fur coat wasn't so thick.

Riach put a tin cup of water near my muzzle. "Drink," he said, checking my pulse and cleaning the wound on my head. "It was not a big knock ye got between yer ears. I should know—I gave it to ye." Then he left me alone again.

I lay there, staring blankly into the darkness, wishing sleep would take me away once more. Rats scurried around me. I tried to paw them away, but only touched air. My head swam. Were the rats real? Or was my fever making me imagine them?

Later, a hatch above me opened and the glimmer of the lantern shone in like sunlight. I could see the strong, dark beams of the ship that was my prison.

Smelling of brandy and moving unsteadily, Mr. Riach descended the ladder. Behind him was Captain Hoseason.

"See for yourself," Riach told the captain. "He's got a high fever, and no appetite for meat. I want this boy taken out of this hole and put in the forecastle."

"Ye want him moved to the crew's quarters? I forbid it!" the captain said sharply. "He is here—and here is where he shall stay."

I tried to lift my head again, but couldn't. I heard the captain turn abruptly and start up the ladder.

"Ye may have been paid to do murder," Riach said sharply to Hoseason, "but I have not!"

The captain jumped back down. "Mr. Riach, I am a hard man, and one who seeks opportunities to put money in my money purse. But for what ye accuse me of now, I am shocked." The captain bent close to me and looked into my eyes. "If ye say the lad will die—"

"Aye, he will!" said Riach.

All of my senses faded. I vaguely remember my paws being cut free, then having my weak body lifted into someone's arms.

The next time that I was fully awake, I realized that I was in the crew's quarters, in a bunk on some blankets.

The crew's quarters were in a raised portion of the ship in the front, or the stem. It was daylight, and as the ship rolled, a dusty beam of sunlight shone in the window. Although the window was very small, I was delighted to be in a place where I could tell night from day. I was also pleased that I could see most of the deck from where I was.

As I lay there for days getting back my health, I came to know the sailors. They were a rough lot. Some had even sailed with pirates and seen things too terrible to mention. But rough as they were, they occasionally remembered to be kind, and sometimes showed a glimmer of honesty. They even returned my money, which had been divided among them. Though it was a bit less than I had had originally, I was glad to get it back.

Most days from then on, the *Covenant* met with head winds—winds blowing against the stem, trying to push her back. The gusts caused huge waves, called swells, which pounded steadily at the ship, one right after another.

The ship tossed up and down as it hit those waves head-on. The hatch that led from the crew's quarters to the deck was usually shut to keep the water out. I was never allowed to set foot on deck. However, I watched the crew come and go, for the sails had to be adjusted every hour to keep us on course. Tempers grew short. Growling and quarreling seemed to travel from man to man. Boy, was I ready for a change!

Unfortunately, the change that occurred was not the one I had in mind. Late one night as I slept with my back to the dim lantern light, I was awakened by whispering. I cocked my ears. With my keen hearing, I heard someone say, "Shuan done it. Beat the boy hard for bringing him food on a dirty pan." Then suddenly two men appeared, carrying the cabin boy, Ransome, in their arms.

I sat up, worried that Mr. Shuan had given Ransome another nasty wound. At that moment the raging sea sent the ship heaving and the lantern swinging. Light fell directly on Ransome's face. His skin was as white as wax. The blood in me ran cold; I drew in my breath as if I'd been struck. Ransome was dead!

Captain Hoseason stepped in and looked sharply around the bunks. He pointed to me. "Come with me," he said. "Ye'll sleep in Ransome's bunk from now on. We want ye to serve in the roundhouse, where the officers live."

"Murderers!" I barked. Using every ounce of strength in all four legs, I pushed past the men. With hopes of escaping, I raced across the decks. Looking out over the sea in the moonlight, I saw no land in sight. Still, I kept running. Suddenly, I slipped and tumbled head-over-tail forward. Two hands reached out and saved me from falling overboard.

I was taken to the roundhouse, which was at the stern, or the rear of the ship. There I was to sleep, and serve Captain Hoseason and his two officers, Mr. Shuan and Mr. Riach. My duties were to bring food, clean, and fetch for three men who I feared and despised! And I knew that Shuan had killed Ransome. I shivered. Ransome had respected these men, and for the most part, he had been faithful. And for that, they'd sent the lad to a watery grave!

I sniffed around. The roundhouse, which was at least six feet above the deck, was quite large. But it was not round—it was a rectangle, with a window in the ceiling, and a door at each end. It lay near the stern, looking out over the main deck, just as the crew's quarters did at the stem. This room contained a table and bench, and two bunks. One was for the captain; the other was for the two mates to use in shifts. Lockers ran from floor to ceiling, and were used to stow away the officers' belongings and some of the ship's supplies—mostly tools and more rope. A second storeroom sat underneath the roundhouse. A single hatchway in the floor led down to the room, which stored all the best meat and drink. This storeroom also contained all of the firearms and gunpowder. A few swords hung in a rack on the wall, but most of the crew's swords were stored elsewhere.

The next day I was thrown into my duties. I had to serve the meals, which the captain ate with the officer who was off duty. Then I had to clean up their mess. By that time the other officer was finished with his shift of standing watch and was ready to eat. So I had to feed him. And one of them was always ordering me to fetch this, or fetch that. My three masters were working me to the bone. But I was afraid to think about what would become of me if I didn't obey them.

At night I slept on a blanket thrown on the deck at one end of the roundhouse, right in the draft of the door. Did I say *slept?* Ha! It was a hard, cold bed, and someone was always waking me up to get him a drink. Two, sometimes all three, would sit down and drink together. They were as noisy as a pack of locked-up hounds!

As for Mr. Shuan, his mind was troubled. I never saw him in his proper wits again. I guessed it was because of his crime.

Ransome's murder weighed heavily on my mind, too. I couldn't help but wonder if and when these men planned to do away with me.

For more than a week, the *Covenant* fought bad weather. Some days she made little headway; others, she was actually pushed backward.

On the afternoon of the tenth day, the conditions were the worst I'd ever seen. Crashing swells washed over the ship, while a thick, white fog hid one end of the ship from the other. Whenever I went on deck, I saw men and officers listening hard for breakers—which I learned were waves crashing into foam against the shore. The presence of breakers would mean we were near land. I didn't hear any myself, but I did smell danger in the air.

At about ten o'clock that night, my nose proved to be right. As I served Mr. Riach and the captain their supper, the ship struck something and made a great ripping sound. I nearly dropped the captain's pan of food. Voices sang out on deck. My two masters leaped to their feet.

"Is she stuck, sir?" cried Mr. Riach.

"No," said the captain, getting up and stepping out the door. "We've only run down a small ship."

We've only run down a small ship?! I thought. I shook my head in disbelief and raced after the captain. He was correct. In the fog, we'd run down a small ship—she'd split in two and was sinking to the bottom of the sea with all her crew. One man, who turned out to be the only passenger aboard to survive the disaster, was dangling from the bowsprit, the pole sticking out from the stem. Amazingly, the man's fancy feathered hat was still cocked perfectly on his head.

By hanging onto the sail rigging and stretching as far as they could, the men aboard the *Covenant* helped bring the survivor onto the main deck of our ship. Then the captain took him to the roundhouse. I followed at their heels.

The man was at least ten years older than my seventeen years, and nimble as a goat. I found out later that he'd saved himself by leaping up and grabbing our bowsprit the instant the two ships collided. He was not tall, and his face, heavily freckled and pitted with smallpox scars, looked tough, yet kind. He wore fancy, costly clothes. His dark hat had a feather, and his pants were made of expensive fabric. When he took off his coat, which was blue and trimmed in white, with silver buttons, he laid a pair of fine silver-mounted pistols on the table. I saw then that he was belted with a great sword. When he spoke, his manners were as elegant as his outfit.

I wagged my tail as I stared up at this fellow. This was a man I'd rather call my friend than my enemy!

"I'm sorry about the boat," said the captain. "Were the crewmen friends of yers?"

The man sighed sadly. "Ye have none such friends in your country. They were as loyal as dogs. They would have died for me."

Wow! As loyal as dogs. Now, those were some great men! I thought.

"I need to get to France, sir," said the gentleman.

The captain eyed him accusingly. "Ye've a French soldier's coat upon yer back, but a Scottish tongue in yer head."

The man smoothed his clothes. "I am a Scottish Highlander," he said, his eyes lighting up proudly. "From the Appin region. But I live in France. There are too many men in Scotland who would like to see me dead."

Yes, I thought, *most everyone who is a loyal follower of King George.*

The Highlander removed the money belt from his waist and poured out two coins upon the table. "Set me ashore where I was intending to go, and I'll reward ye for yer trouble."

"France, I cannot do," said the captain. "But I can take ye up Linnhe Loch and get ye to yer Appin country-side." He rubbed his chin. "Linnhe Loch's a very narrow inlet, and my ship is big. Ye'll have to pay a good amount for placing my ship in such danger."

I listened as the captain drove up the price.

"Very well," said the gentleman finally. "It's a deal."

Now I knew where we were headed!

The captain went out rather hurriedly and left me alone with the stranger.

Using my teeth, I set a pan of meat before him. I would have loved to grab a bite, but didn't. "Ye're a rebel supporter of Prince Charles?" I said.

"Aye," said he, beginning to eat. "And ye, by yer long face, should be loyal to King George?"

"No. I'm neither for the king, nor rebel. I'm right in between," I said, trying not to annoy him.

He smiled and pointed to a bottle on the table. "Well, Mr.-in-between, this bottle is dry. Could ye get me some drink?"

"I'll go ask for the key," I said, then padded out on deck. The seas had calmed, but the fog was still as thick as porridge. I finally spotted the captain and the two officers. They stood with their heads together, under the ship's bell. Instinct told me they were up to no good. I hid behind a coil of rope and pricked up my ears.

"Trouble is," the captain said, "all our guns are in the roundhouse under this man's nose. The powder, too."

"Couldn't we trick him into coming out of the roundhouse?" Mr. Riach cried out, as if hitting upon a sudden thought.

"He's better where he is," said Hoseason. "On the main deck he'd have too much room to use his sword."

"True," said Riach, "but he's hard to attack when he is in the roundhouse."

I heard Hoseason sigh. "We can get the man talking," he said. "Surround him. Then we can pin him by the arms. If that doesn't work, we can ram him into a wall

before he has time to draw. One way or another, we shall do him in. That money belt will be ours."

I was so angry I almost howled outright. However, fear of these greedy, bloodthirsty men kept me quiet. Silently, I turned and crept back to the roundhouse.

With a paw, I reached out and gently touched the stranger's arm. "Do ye want to be killed?"

He sprang to his feet and gave me a questioning look.

I cried, "They're all murderers here—it's a ship full of them! They've murdered a cabin boy already. Now it's yer turn."

"Aye, aye, I see what ye mean," said he, looking at me curiously. "And will ye stand with me?"

I pawed the air in agreement. "I will! I am no thief or murderer."

"And yer name?" he asked.

"David Balfour," I said.

"My name is Stewart." He drew himself up proudly. "Same as the Stewart kings. Alan Breck Stewart. But Alan Breck is what they call me."

"Breck" meant "spotted." Alan was given the name because of his pockmarked skin.

He turned and started examining the roundhouse. "Only the window in the ceiling—and the doors at each end—is large enough for a man to fit through."

I trotted over to the door facing the stem. Standing on my hind legs, I tried to slide the lock shut with my front paws.

"No, no." Alan stopped me. "Leave the door open. Then I'll know where my enemies are." He drew his great sword and practiced wielding it in the room. "I must stick to the point," he said, taking note of the table. "A pity. How many men are there aboard, David?"

I counted twice in my mind to be sure. "Fifteen."

Sighing, Alan put a powder horn, a bag of ammunition, and all the pistols that he had gathered from the storeroom on the table in front of me.

"But I don't have much experience firing a gun," I told him.

"Then ye shall load the pistols with powder and bullets for me, and watch the closed door for signs of entry. We'll make a soldier of ye yet, David." He half-smiled. "What else have ye to guard?"

"There's the window above us, Mr. Stewart. But I would need eyes on both sides of my head in order to watch that, too!"

"True," said Alan. "But have ye no ears?"

"Yes!" I barked out excitedly. "I would hear the breaking of the glass!"

I sat at the table and readied the pistols, keeping my eyes and ears alert. My chest was tight underneath my fur, and my mouth was as dry as a sun-bleached bone. The thought of the numbers that were soon to leap in upon us kept my heart pounding. I was sure I'd be dead by morning.

Chapter Six

S uddenly Captain Hoseason showed his face at the door we were guarding.

"Stand guard!" cried Alan, and he pointed his sword at Hoseason.

The captain neither flinched nor drew back a foot. "A naked sword?" said he. "This is a very strange way to return my hospitality."

Hospitality? I thought. *Somebody had better get this guy a dictionary!* Hoseason's officers stood behind him looking like Dobermans waiting to pounce.

"I see yer men at your back, sir!" said Alan. "My sword has slashed the heads off more of King George's soldiers than ye have toes upon yer feet. The sooner the clash begins, the sooner ye'll taste this steel through yer stomach."

The captain said nothing to Alan, but turned to me and scowled as if I'd bitten him. The next moment he was gone.

My heartbeat quickened. I heard a rush of feet, a roar, then a shout. Suddenly, Mr. Shuan stood in the doorway, crossing blades with Alan.

"That's the one who killed the cabin boy!" I cried.

"Look to yer window!" said Alan. Before I turned away, I saw Alan pass his sword through the first mate's body. An icy shiver raced down my back.

My head was barely back at the window when five men, carrying a large piece of wood, ran at the closed door. *Bam!* The door shook, but held to its hinges. Then the men backed up to make ready for another attempt to break it down.

I had never fired a pistol in my life. Just as the men swung the hefty piece of wood forward, I fired the pistol into the air. I must have hit a man, because someone yowled like a cat. Before the crewmen had time to recover from the assault, I picked up another pistol and sent a second shot over their heads. Then, after I had fired my third shot, the whole group dropped the wood plank and ran for cover.

Scaredy cats! I thought.

I looked through the pistol smoke toward Alan. He stood there as before, but now his sword was running with blood. On the floor in front of him was Mr. Shuan, dead.

"There's one of yer king's subjects for ye!" cried Alan, as men reached down and dragged Mr. Shuan out of the roundhouse. He turned to me. "They'll be back again. Keep an eye out, David."

I returned to reloading the pistols I had fired. I kept my eyes open and my ears alert. Until that moment, I'd been too busy to be frightened. With everything suddenly still, fear raced through my veins. Visions of sharp swords and cold steel chewed at my mind.

I stood rigid and perked up my ears. I heard mutterings, and footsteps, and the brushing of clothing against the outside wall—all on Alan's side of the roundhouse. Then

I heard someone drop softly onto the roof above me. My heart pounded. The men were taking their places in the dark.

Someone cried out a signal and men rushed toward the door. At the same moment, the glass in the window crashed into a thousand pieces. A man leaped through the opening and landed on the floor. Before he could move again, I grabbed a pistol and pointed it at him. But I could not pull the trigger. He was a living, breathing creature, just as I was—okay, maybe not as nice. But he did have one good quality—he was loyal, even if it was to the likes of the captain.

Swearing, the man sliced the air in front of me with his sword. Then he reached out and caught me by the back of my neck. I knew his next move would do me in. I fired into his middle. He groaned, then fell to the floor. Another man's legs dangled through the broken window. Snatching up another pistol, I shot this crew member as he jumped toward me. His shirt reddened; he dropped in a heap. I stared in horror—I had killed two men. Yet they'd left me no choice.

"David!" Alan shouted for help, bringing me to my senses. One of the seamen had caught him and clung to his body like a leech. Alan was fighting him with a knife in one hand and swinging his sword in the other to hold off another sailor who'd broken into the roundhouse. More faces crowded together at the doorway. My heart sank. How could we survive this attack?

I grabbed my sword, but I had no time to be of help. The man hanging onto Alan finally fell limply to the deck. Alan, leaping back to get his distance, ran upon the others like a bull, roaring as he went. They turned to escape, but stumbled and fell against one another as they tried to run. Alan was now out on the main deck. The sword in his hands flashed again and again. With every slash there came the howl of a man being hurt. Alan drove our enemies back along the main deck in the same way a sheepdog would herd sheep.

Alan came back to the roundhouse puffing out his chest as if he'd just won the blue ribbon for Best of Show. I heard the seamen still running and crying out as if Alan were still behind them in hot pursuit. Then I heard them tumble one upon another into the crew's quarters, and shut the hatch.

Looking around the roundhouse, I felt faint. Three men lay dead on the floor inside, another at the door.

Alan came to me with open arms and embraced me. "I love ye like a brother, David. And, oh, man," he cried proudly, "aren't I a great fighter?"

I pawed the air in agreement as Alan rolled the bodies out of the roundhouse. *Yes,* I thought, *ye're a fine fighter.* But as I looked at the dead men, a feeling of sadness crept through me. Yet I knew we had no choice but to do what we did. These were men sent to kill us.

Alan clapped my shoulder. "Ye were a brave lad. Now sleep. I'll take the first watch."

I looked around, checking for a glass-free spot on the floor as the ship rolled with the motion of the sea.

"Ye did right by me, David," said Alan, watching me with admiration. "I wouldn't trade ye for all of Appin." His eyes twinkled brightly when he mentioned the region of his homeland.

Not until later, when I learned how dearly Alan loved his Appin kin, did I realize just how much his words meant.

I wagged my tail and then curled up in the corner near the door that had been kept shut. I slept until Alan woke me up three hours later. Yawning, I stood up and stretched out my back legs.

Nothing stirred during my watch, and by the banging of the helm, I knew that the seamen had no one at the tiller to steer the ship. Too many men were dead or injured, I supposed.

Hearing a great number of gulls crying around the ship, I figured we must have drifted fairly close to a coastline. We were lucky that the night was windless, or the ship might have run aground.

It began to rain. Looking out through the drops of water, I saw the great stone hills of Skye nearby. I knew the Island of Skye was off the northwest coast of Scotland. That meant since leaving my uncle, the ship had sailed from the east side of Scotland to the west. Wow!

In the morning over breakfast, Alan and I smiled at our success in keeping control of the roundhouse.

While Alan brushed breakfast crumbs off his coat, I looked around. "All the good food and drink are at our disposal!" My tail thumped. "Now those thirsty sailors will have to drink water instead of liquor."

Sampling a fine biscuit, Alan nodded. "We'll hear more from those vermin before long, David. Depend on it. There are still eleven of them breathing. Ye may keep a man from the fighting, but never from his bottle."

Smiling, and taking a knife from the table, Alan cut off one of the silver buttons from his coat.

"I got these from my father, Duncan Stewart. Now I give ye one of them to be a keepsake for last night's work." He put it on the table in front of me. "Wherever ye go and show that button, the friends of Alan Breck will come to yer aid."

Boy, this Duncan guy sure sounded like he must be an important person! I was so honored by Alan's action that I was completely speechless. Then, carefully picking up the button in my teeth, I dropped it into the money

purse that hung on my neck. Though I didn't know it then, the button would one day help me.

Soon Mr. Riach motioned to us from the deck. I took a pistol and waited for him to speak.

"The captain wants to meet with yer friend."

"And how do we know that it's not more trickery?" I cried.

Mr. Riach shook his head. "He means none, Davie. And if he did, I'll tell ye the honest truth, he could not get the men to follow his orders."

I discussed the proposal with Alan, and we agreed to meet with the captain. But Mr. Riach did not turn and go. Instead, he begged me for a drink of liquor.

"No, no." I shook my head until my ears flopped.

"Please, Davie. Remember, it was I who took ye from the hold of the ship and nursed ye back to health."

"Aye." His words tugged at my heart. Tipping a bottle, I poured a few ounces of liquor into a cup.

Mr. Riach drank some, then carried the rest away, to share, I suppose, with the captain.

A little later, as agreed, the captain came to one of the windows. He stood there in the rain with his arm in a sling. He looked so pale and old that I actually felt sorry for him. Alan held a pistol in his lap.

"Ye've made a mess of my ship," said the captain, frowning. "I haven't enough men left to work her, and my first officer, the navigator, is dead. We know we are south of the Island of Skye, but none of the rest of us knows how to navigate around the coastline of the island of Mull. But I know it's one that's very dangerous to ships. Could ye direct us at all?"

"It's doubtful," said Alan. "I'm more of a fighting man—as ye have seen for yourself—than a sailor. But I've been picked up and set down often upon this coast, and I should know something about it. I'll help if I can."

Still frowning, the captain nodded.

"And now," said Alan, "as I hear ye're a little short of brandy, I'll offer ye a change—a bottle of brandy for two buckets of fresh water."

Captain Hoseason agreed eagerly.

When the water was brought to us, Alan and I drank thirstily and used some of it to wash the mess from the roundhouse floor. Outside, a breeze came up, blowing away the rain and bringing out the sun. Everything was glistening—especially the mountainous islands that rose up on both sides of us.

In the afternoon, Alan and I sat in the freshly cleaned roundhouse, with the doors open at each end. As Alan puffed away on one of the captain's pipes, I told him all about my misfortunes. He listened carefully, nodding at all the right times. Only when I mentioned my friend, Mr. Campbell the minister, did Alan speak up.

"I hate all by that name!" cried he. "Campbells are on the side of King George."

"Why, he is a man ye should be proud to know," said I.

"I've said it before, and I'll say it again," said he. "I know nothing I would help a Campbell to, unless it was a bullet. I would hunt them like rats. If I lay dying in my bed, I would crawl upon my knees to my window to aim a shot at one."

"Alan!" I cried, wagging my tail nervously. "Why do ye hate the Campbells?"

"Ye know very well that I am an Appin Stewart, and the Campbells have long attacked and killed members of my clan."

A *clan* is a group—like the Scottish Highlanders—made up of households who claim to be descendants from the same family line.

"And the Campbells were given our lands by the order of King George!" he cried loudly, slamming his fist upon the table.

I was beginning to understand how deeply this rebel felt about his cause.

"The king had lying words, lying documents, and tricks fit for a peddler." Alan shook his head. "Even I was tricked by him at first. That is how I came to enlist in the English army. A black spot upon my character, to be sure. However, I eventually deserted and switched to the right side—the side that is trying to put a Scotsman on the English throne."

Desertion is punishable by death, I thought. "Good heavens, man!" I cried, putting my paw on the table. "Ye are a rebel, a deserter, and a soldier in the French king's army. Those are three reasons why King George and all his loyal subjects in Scotland want ye dead. What tempts ye to come back into this country?"

Alan sighed. "I miss my friends and homeland. Scotland is where my heart is, even when I'm in France." He waved his pipe stem in the air. "But more important, I have come back to collect money to help the great men of the Highlands who have been driven out by the Red Fox." Alan clamped his jaw shut the very moment he mentioned the name; his face turned grim.

"And who is the Red Fox?" I asked, a little frightened, but curious.

Alan laid down the pipe, which he had long since let go out. "The Red Fox is Colin Roy Campbell, a red-haired scoundrel—one of King George's men." Alan stopped to swallow down his anger like a hunk of sharp bone. "Red Fox is the man who was sent to take away the farms of the Highlanders when King George gave all of their land to the Campbells. But my kinsmen hung on to their land!"

"Terrific!" I flipped in the air. "The Red Fox was beaten. And although I'm not a rebel, I'm surely glad he was beaten."

"Him beaten?" echoed Alan. "No, no. It's little ye know of the Campbells, and less of the Red Fox. He will not be beaten till his blood's dripping on the hillsides! And if I ever hold him at a gun's end, the Lord have pity upon him!"

I put a paw on the table. "It's not the Red Fox who tries to ruin your people. It's the king. And if ye killed this man today, there would be another in his shoes tomorrow, doing the same job."

Alan's face reddened with emotion. "Ye're a good lad in a fight. But, my friend, ye don't understand!"

71

I thought it was wise to change the subject before he unleashed his anger again. So I asked him questions about himself. Was that ever a mistake! Brag! Brag! Brag! Brag! Brag! I learned that Alan was skilled in playing all kinds of music, was a poet, and had read books in both French and English. He also said that he was a good fisherman, a great shot, and an excellent fencer.

As I listened, I hoped Alan's bark was worse than his bite. Otherwise, when he saw Red Fox, Alan would add "murderer" to his list of unlawful doings.

Joe's doings aren't unlawful, but he did leave the house when he wasn't supposed to. Will he get back home in time to finish cleaning up the garage, or will Ellen arrive first? Let's get on back to Oakdale and find out.

Chapter Seven

Joe felt really good about the camp site he had selected in Jackson Park. He checked his watch as he and Wishbone started for home. "I hope Mom is running late." He broke into a jog as he chose the shortest trail out of the park. "Come on, Wishbone. We've got to hurry."

Wishbone ran alongside Joe until they reached their cul-de-sac. Wishbone stopped and eyed Wanda's driveway. "Ahhh . . . no car. Nobody's home." He trotted into her yard and sniffed her trees and flowers, in search of a good place to dig for bones. "Wishbone's Adventures in Wandaland!"

"Come on, Wishbone," Joe called, panting. "You know Miss Gilmore doesn't like you messing around in her yard."

"But she has the best yard in the neighborhood! Wait a minute, Joe, and I'll give it the canine seal of approval."

Joe glanced over his shoulder. "Come on, boy."

Wishbone hurried after Joe. "Catch you guys later," he said, cutting between two of the decorative flamingos in Wanda's yard.

When Wishbone reached his garage, Joe was again sorting items into the piles in the driveway. After a quick snoop in the yard, Wishbone jumped up into the lawn chair.

"Well, if I can't have any cookies"—he turned to eye Wanda's lawn again—"and I can't have an adventure, I might as well have a nap." He started to put his head down, but he heard a familiar noise and sat up. Ellen's station wagon was coming down the street. Wishbone barked. "'Mom' alert, Joe."

Joe was rummaging through a cardboard box as Ellen parked by the curb. "Hi, Joe," Ellen said, climbing out.

"Hi." Using the bottom of his T-shirt, Joe wiped the sweat from his face. He pulled an old pirate costume from the box and held it up in front of him. "I can't believe this used to fit me."

"Well, it did." Looking at the piles in the driveway, Ellen smiled. "It sure looks like you two have been working hard." She glanced at Wishbone in the lawn chair. "Okay, maybe just *one* of you."

"Hey, it's the law," Wishbone said. "Even supervisors get breaks now and then." He put his head on his paws. "Uh . . . did you get the ginger snaps, Ellen? All this work takes a lot out of a dog."

Ellen grabbed a bundle of groceries from the backseat and motioned with her head. "Come on, Joe. It looks like you could use a break."

Sighing, Wishbone rolled his eyes toward Ellen. "Nobody listens to the dog."

Joe fidgeted. "Really, Mom, I should stay here and finish this."

Ellen glanced over her shoulder as she walked toward the doorway. "Oh, come on. I'm proud of you for staying home to get this done, Joe. I have a half gallon of raspberry-twist ice cream in this bag to prove it."

Wishbone jumped out of the chair and trotted after her. "Did someone mention ice cream?"

Joe looked embarrassed and dropped his glance to the ground. "Sure, I'll have some, Mom." He grabbed the other two bags from the car and then carried them to the kitchen.

While Joe went to wash up, Wishbone sat on the kitchen floor and watched Ellen put away the groceries.

He moved closer to the counter when she dished out two bowls of ice cream. *Hmm . . .* Wishbone thought. *Let me guess which one of us doesn't get a bowl.*

Joe came into the kitchen and sat down at the table. Trotting to his side, Wishbone waited patiently.

"It looked like you were nearly finished with the garage." Ellen sounded quite pleased. She set the bowls on the table, giving the fuller one to Joe.

"Yeah, I guess so." Joe stared into his bowl.

"I'm sure Wanda, being president of the historical society and owner of the *Chronicle,* will appreciate your efforts." Ellen took a mouthful of ice cream. "Her goal, and the society's, is to someday earn enough money to buy one of the older houses in Oakdale to use as a museum. Then the society could keep its headquarters at the *Chronicle,* but move its artifacts to the house."

Joe nodded. For a while the two ate without a sound, except for the clinking of the spoons against their bowls.

"Helllooo! If you look at the floor, you'll notice the dog is looking quite cute."

Ellen put her last spoonful of ice cream into her mouth. "Mmm . . . so good." She stood and headed to the sink. "You know, since you stuck it out all afternoon like

I asked you to, Joe, I'll finish up the garage. I have to sort through a few of my things, anyway."

Joe looked up in surprise. "That's okay, Mom. I can do it. I don't mind." He stood.

Ellen shook her head as she tried to scrape out one last spoonful of ice cream from her bowl. "It'll only take me a few minutes. And I know you've been excited about this camping trip. Go ahead, start your planning." She grinned. "Consider it time off for good behavior."

Sighing, Joe flopped back down into his chair. He stirred his raspberry twist ice cream, then put his dish down for Wishbone.

Wishbone looked at it and wagged his tail. "Wow! I get all this? Thanks, pal!" He looked up at Joe. "Oh." His tail drooped. "I guess you lost your appetite because you're feeling guilty about leaving the house this afternoon

before cleaning the garage. You should have told Ellen the truth, Joe. You'd feel better. Works every time."

Wishbone cocked his head.

"I could've explained it to her, Joe, but she never listens to me." Looking back at the dish, he wagged his tail just a bit. "No use wasting the ice cream." He sank his muzzle into the bowl and set his tongue to work. "Mmm-mmm! Pass the whipped cream and nuts."

The doorbell rang. Wishbone's head popped up.

"Wanda alert."

Licking the ice cream from his nose, he inched closer to Joe. He heard Ellen open the front door, then cocked his head and listened some more.

"And if my nose and ears are correct—which they always are—David is here, too."

Ellen's face was serious when she came into the kitchen with Wanda and David. "Wanda was just telling me that there's been a little trouble in town."

"What kind of trouble?" Joe asked.

Wanda's hands moved through the air as she talked. "My friend Marge called and said someone scrawled graffiti on the front windows at the *The Oakdale Chronicle*. They painted the words 'Rummage Sale Canceled' all over the windows. Isn't that terrible?" she said. "Why would anyone want to do that?"

She took a quick breath, then hurried on.

"Well, someone said they saw somebody who looked like Curtis hanging around this afternoon." She nodded to emphasize her words.

Wishbone circled the floor and then lay down. "Careful, there, Wanda. I myself have been unjustly accused of turning over garbage cans."

Wanda rested her hands on her hips. "Someone is going to be in big trouble for this." Tilting her head, she looked at Ellen. "I'm surprised you didn't hear about it. It just happened about a half hour ago. Weren't you at the library?"

Wishbone gasped and jumped up. "Joe! They're blaming the wrong guy! Tell them! Curtis was in the park at the time."

Ellen squinted in thought. "I was probably getting groceries."

Joe fidgeted. "That's too bad about the windows, Miss Gilmore."

David nodded in agreement. "I'll say."

"Got your camping stuff ready?" Joe changed the subject.

Looking a bit surprised by the shift in the conversation, David shook his head. "Did you and Wishbone find anything this afternoon?"

Joe's eyes darted to Ellen, then back to David. "You mean while I was cleaning out the garage? Just things I don't use anymore. Oh, and my camping stuff." He jumped up from his chair and hurried to the doorway. "Come on. Let's go to my room. I'll show you."

Ellen and Wanda looked at Joe curiously.

Joe glanced back. "What?"

"I think they're surprised by your reaction, Joe," Wishbone said. "You changed the subject so quickly. . . . Aren't you going to tell them about seeing Curtis?"

"Uh . . . nothing," Wanda said, gently shaking her head as she exchanged looks with Ellen.

David followed Joe up the stairs. "I don't have much time. I just came to see if you found us a campsite."

"I'll get to the bottom of this yet," Wishbone said, climbing the steps after them. "Or is that the top?" He trotted into Joe's room and jumped on the bed. David sat down beside him.

"I picked out a great spot, not too far from the tire swing." Joe slung his backpack up next to them, opened it wide, and began stuffing things in—a jacket, a deck of cards, some travel games . . .

"What's wrong, Joe?" David asked, as he scratched Wishbone behind his ears. "You're acting weird."

Taking a deep breath, Joe pushed the hair off his forehead. "I wasn't supposed to leave the house this afternoon and look for a site, so I did it while my mom was in town shopping. Curtis couldn't have been the one to write on the windows—I saw him at the park at the very moment that was happening."

"So why didn't you tell the truth?" David asked.

Joe plopped down on the bed and rolled a piece of lint between his fingers. "If Mom finds out I went to the park instead of cleaning out the garage, I'll probably get grounded. That'd mean good-bye to the camping trip. And after what Curtis did to us . . ."

"Bingo! To save Curtis, you'd have to sacrifice yourself." Wishbone pawed the air. "That's a tough one. But if you don't speak out, Curtis could get in deep trouble. *And* he didn't do it."

David raised his brows. "So what are you going to do, Joe?"

"Why should I ruin my last weekend before school starts for Curtis? When I saw him this afternoon, he made it sound like getting the bikes locked together was our own fault—as if we started the trouble by not letting him and Damont cut in line at Pepper Pete's."

"I'm glad I'm not in your shoes, Joe. I wish I could stay and help you, but I need to get home." David checked his watch, then stood. "My parents are going to see an early movie, then to have dinner, and it's my job to baby-sit Emily."

"That's okay. See you tomorrow." Joe smiled.

But Wishbone could tell it wasn't a real smile. It was the kind people wore when they wanted to pretend everything was okay—even when it wasn't.

There is a real battle going on inside Joe. But it is nothing like the one David Balfour and the *Covenant* are about to have with Mother Nature.

Chapter Eight

Late that night, when Alan and I were both dozing, I was awakened by the sound of footsteps.

Hoseason poked his head into the roundhouse doorway and spoke to Alan. "Come out and see if ye can help navigate the ship, sir."

"Is this one of yer tricks?" asked Alan, sitting up.

"No tricks!" cried the captain. "We'll soon be rounding the southwest coast of the island of Mull. My ship's in danger!"

By the concerned look on his face and the sharpness of his voice, it was plain to both of us the captain was telling the truth. We scrambled out on deck.

I looked off the port side but couldn't see the island, even though the moon was full and bright. I shivered. The night was bitter cold. The wind blew so hard it made even my short fur stand on end.

And it was rough sailing for the *Covenant*. She creaked and groaned as if she were haunted. Pitching and straining, the ship tore through the seas at a great rate, chased by the westerly waves. We all spread our feet apart to try to balance ourselves.

Suddenly the ship rose on a high swell. "Look!" Captain Hoseason pointed off the starboard side.

A formation like a fountain rose out of the moonlit sea, and immediately afterward we heard a low roaring.

"What do ye call that?" asked the captain gloomily.

"The sea breaking on rocks—a reef." Alan hugged his coat tighter to him. "And it's good we know where it is."

I may not be a sea dog—what sailors call a seaman with a lot of experience—but I'd been on ship long enough to pick up some of the seafaring slang; I knew a reef was a chain of jagged rocks near the surface of the water—a real hazard for a ship!

"Aye," said Hoseason, "if it's the only one." As he spoke, a second fountain shot up farther to the south. "There!" He pointed. "If I had a chart, or if Shuan had been spared, my ship would not be in such danger! What do ye say?"

As I looked at Alan, a gust of wind caught my ears and flipped them back. Whoa! I turned my head and let the wind right them again.

"I think," said Alan, "that'll be another reef."

The captain squinted into the night. "Are there many of them?"

"Truly, sir, I'm no navigator," said Alan. "But if my memory is correct, there are ten miles of them off the tip of the island."

I heard footsteps. Mr. Riach joined us.

The captain exchanged glances with him, then looked back at Alan. "There's a way through the rocks, I suppose?"

"I'm sure," said Alan, his teeth chattering. His brow pulled together. "And somehow, I think if we stay close to the shore of Mull, we'll pass through the rocks unharmed."

I blew on my front paws and rubbed them together

in an attempt to warm them. It was useless. Shivering, I crouched lower to the deck.

The captain braced himself against the wind. "Well, we're in for it now." He stuck his hands into his armpits for warmth. "Mr. Riach, we'll have to come as near the tip of the island of Mull as we can take her."

With that, Captain Hoseason snapped an order to the steersman, then sent Riach up the mast as lookout. Including the officers, there were only five men on deck who were fit and willing to work, and two of them were injured.

"The sea to the south is thick with rocks!" shouted Riach, his clothes flapping in the wind like flags. "It does seem clearer in by the land."

"Well, sir," said Hoseason to Alan, "we'll stick with yer way. But I think I might do as well if I were to trust a blind man."

It turned out the captain was right. As we neared the southern tip of Mull, the reefs began to show up right in our path. Sometimes Mr. Riach cried down to us to change the ship's course. Sometimes his call came barely soon enough. One reef was so close to our side that when the sea slammed against it, the spray fell on us like rain.

I shook, ridding my coat of the salt water. My two-legged companions, unskilled in the art of shaking off water, had to suffer more than I.

The tide at the southern tip of Mull was so strong that it threw the ship about. The captain made his way to the helm to help steer the ship. He leaned on the lever, adding his weight to the two seamen already struggling against it. Together the three of them fought to keep the ship on course.

Glancing about in the brightness of the night, I saw the reefs. For the first time, I realized what terrible danger we were in. Oh! I closed my eyes and tucked my tail between my legs. The ship rolled to the side, sending me tumbling. Alan reached out and caught me by the back of my neck. *I wish I were on land, anywhere!* I thought.

Finally, Mr. Riach shouted down that he saw clear water ahead.

Yes! I thought.

"Ye were right, sir," Hoseason said, nodding at Alan. "Ye have saved my ship."

But no sooner had the captain spoken than Mr. Riach cried out again in distress. "Reef to windward! Reef to windward!"

And at that very instant the tide caught the ship. She spun in the wind like a top. We crashed into the reef so hard that all of us on deck landed flat. Above us, Mr. Riach swung dangerously from the rigging.

"Hold on!" I barked. Scrambling to my four feet in a second, I ran to assist him. As I fought to hold the rigging steady with my teeth, he climbed down quickly to the deck. Then he and the other seamen ran over and began to lower the rowboat.

Alan and I helped, too. It was hard work supporting the rowboat, while at the same time untying the ropes that secured it to the ship. Lucky for me I'd played so many games of tug-of-war. *Bam!* Another swell broke over us. Cries went out.

I glanced around. The captain stood, staring out to sea, speechless.

Somehow the captain managed to stay on his feet. The wind howled and the sails scraped, and the crashing spray flew through the moonlight!

Each wave hammered the ship farther onto the reef, grinding her to pieces as if she were kibble. Steadying the rowboat with my paws, I looked across at the shore.

"What part of Scotland is that—Highlands or Lowlands?" I barked at Alan over the roar of the wind and the sea.

His face was grim. "The worst possible for me—the Lowlands, filled with Campbells and other sympathizers of King George."

As we started to lift the rowboat over the side, a shrill cry split the air. "For God's sake, everybody hold on!"

I hunkered down and dug my nails into the deck. A swell so huge followed that it lifted the ship right up as if it were a toy. Then the vessel came crashing down on her side. A loose barrel rammed into my shoulder, and my paws flew up. I fell overboard and dropped into the cold sea.

I went down, swallowed water, and came up. I saw a blink of the moon, then sank again. All the while I was being dragged along, beaten and choked by the waves. I felt as if the sea had swallowed me whole.

As I bobbed up again, a loose piece of wood from the ship nearly hit my head. I grabbed for it with my front paws but missed. On the second try I got it and held on for dear life.

Hanging onto the wood wasn't easy. I was shivering terribly and nearly numb from the icy water. I knew I could not survive the cold of the sea for long.

Suddenly I was tossed about again, sank, then came up sputtering. But for some reason I could not explain, I'd landed in a pool of water without waves. Finally, some good luck! Bubbles gently frothed up around me. What this was, I had no clue. At another time the bubbles might be fun to bite into and pop, but right at that moment I had little energy to spare.

Looking around, I was amazed to see how far I'd traveled from the ship. I howled for help, but the ship was too far away. She was still holding together, but I

couldn't see whether or not the crew had been able to launch the rowboat.

The shore of Earraid, a small island at the tip of Mull, was close. In the moonlight I could see the dots of heather, and the sparkling of the mica in the rocks. Hmm . . . I didn't know how to swim, but I had to try to reach the shore. I held onto the wood with my front paws, stretched out my hind legs, and kicked. It was hard work, but after about an hour I was close enough to let go of the wood and dogpaddle to shore.

Land! I belly-crawled onto the sand and collapsed. "Thank ye! Thank ye!" I panted.

When I finally raised my muzzle and looked around, however, my heart sank. I had never seen a place so barren and deserted. The land was wet marsh, where nothing grew except heather bushes.

After resting, I sniffed around, hoping to find something or someone. Not one track. Nothing but shellfish! I pried open some of the shells with my teeth and ate the clamlike things inside. *Blech!* I should have suspected as much. After all, cats love seafood.

Soon my stomach churned like the very sea that had cast me here. I leaned over and gave the small shellfish right back to the sea. . . .

The next three days were horrible. I was sick, and it rained nonstop. Thoughts of my uncle and how I would get even with him kept me going.

I shivered and shook, shivered and shook. I didn't know my fur could hold so much water! I could see some chimney smoke rising in the distance on the island of Mull, but I couldn't figure out how to get over there from my island. I paced so much my paws hurt. Even licking them didn't help.

So there I was, marooned on Earraid. On three sides

of me lay the sea. On the fourth side, the side that separated me from Mull, the seawater flowed like a river current. Twice I tried to dogpaddle across, but the current was too strong and the sea-river too wide. Weak from hunger and cold, I had to turn back.

I kept wandering. Often my thoughts drifted to Alan. Was he still alive? I could only hope so. . . . I searched my money purse. Some of my coins had been lost at sea, but at least I still had Alan's treasured button.

One night as I drifted off to sleep, I remembered the wish I'd made during my last moments on the *Covenant*. It had come true—I was on land. Yet I was still doomed.

The next morning I felt better, so I went for an early walk. It was low tide and I thought I might find some new kind of food. In about half an hour I came to the side of the island that was across from Mull. The water was not as deep as it had been the day before. I couldn't believe it! It had shrunk to a little trickle. Then I realized it was that way because it was low tide. If I'd been a sea dog, I would have figured out that high-tide-low-tide thing right away. Tail wagging, I crossed over to Mull, barely getting my paws wet.

Right away I saw Mull was rugged—full of prickly bushes, marsh grasses, and big stones. Maybe there were roads for men who knew the countryside well, but my nose would be my guide. I headed straight for the smoke I had seen.

Hours later I found it. The smoke rose from a stone house at the bottom of a valley. Out front a humbly dressed old man sat smoking his pipe in the sun. He spoke Gaelic—the language spoken by the people of the Scottish Highlands—but he knew enough English to tell me my shipmates had gotten to shore.

"Was one of the crew dressed like a gentleman?" I asked the elderly fellow.

"They all wore sailors' trousers except for one. He wore breeches and stockings and a fine hat."

"Alan is alive!" I barked out. Too weak to flip in the air, I walked in a tight circle instead.

The man clapped his hand to his brow. "Ye must be the lad with the silver button!" he cried.

"Yes." How did he know about me? I wondered, pulling the button out of my money purse.

"Well, then," said the old man, "I have words to pass on to ye. Ye are to follow yer friend to the mainland, by way of the ferry."

The man's wife brought me out a dinner of bread and chicken. Then the couple invited me inside to stay the night.

Gratefully, I curled up in a corner on the floor. Their house was thick with smoke and full of more holes than any house I'd ever seen. But it seemed like a palace to me. As I lay there looking into the firelight, I couldn't help but think about the Shaws land and wonder if it was really mine.

Near noon the next day I left the kindly couple. I begged the poor, old gentleman to take some money, but he wouldn't.

Making my way toward the ferry, I passed people digging in fields so worthless that they wouldn't yield enough food even to feed a cat. Still, the farmers were kind enough to point me on my way.

It wasn't until I boarded the ferry to cross to the mainland that my luck again seemed to take a turn for the worse.

Chapter Nine

The skipper of the ferry was Neil Roy Macrob. Alan had told me earlier that "Macrob" was one of the names of his kinsmen. Since Alan himself had sent me here, I was eager to speak privately with Neil Roy. But the boat was crowded, and so I didn't get my chance until we reached the shore of the mainland.

"I am seeking somebody," said I. "And I think ye will have news of him. Alan Breck Stewart is his name." Instead of showing him the silver button, I offered him a coin.

He drew back as if I'd bitten him, and gave me a cold look. "The man ye ask for is in France. But if he were here and ye offered me a mountain of coins, I would not hurt a hair upon his head!" He pointed away. "Now go!"

Wow! Alan's kinsmen had canine-caliber loyalty. A far cry from the treatment I'd received from Ebenezer. "Wait—ye don't understand." I dug out the button from my purse.

"Ah," said Neil, "ye should have shown me that first. If ye are the lad with the silver button, all is well. I have been told to see that ye travel in safety." Pausing, he frowned. "But there are two things ye should never do—

never speak the name 'Alan Breck' out loud, and never offer money to a Highlander gentleman."

"Thank ye for the advice. I will remember next time," I said gratefully.

Hastily, Neil gave me my route that Alan had passed to him. "And after ye get off the ferry," he said, "ask the way to the home of James of the Glens."

Then Neil gave me one last bit of advice.

"Speak with no one on the way so ye will avoid the Campbells and the king's red soldiers. They are looking for Highlander rebels. Leave the road and lie under a bush if ye see anyone coming."

I thanked him, spent the night at an inn, then started off in the morning with my nose to the ground.

Soon the countryside became harsh, and it was difficult to travel. My paws were *so* sore from hiking across the rough rocks. I continued traveling north and arrived at the inlet called Linnhe Loch.

There, I hired a fisherman to take me to the Appin region—the area where Alan was from. It was nearly noon before we set out. The day was dark with clouds, and the sun shone through only upon little patches of sea every now and then. But at least my paws were getting a rest!

As I looked into the distance off both sides of the fishing boat, high mountains rose, like gigantic sharp-edged boulders. They looked black and gloomy under the darkness of the clouds. Appin seemed like a forbidding region, yet Alan told me he loved it with all his heart.

All at once I spied a clump of red uniforms moving along the shore. Then another. Then there came a little flash, as though the sun had struck upon bright steel. Oh, great—King George's soldiers.

"Drop me off further down the shore," I whispered, pointing to a spot.

From the shore I hightailed it up the craggy mountainside, slowing twice to glance over my shoulder. Wow! What a tough climb! Only when I finally reached some trees for cover did I stop to rest. That was when my mind began to fill with doubt. Should I really be going to join a rebel? I wondered.

I put my nose in the air and sniffed for danger. Before long I actually found some! Or, rather, it found me.

I heard horses coming through a wooded area to my left. As I glanced at a turn in the road, three travelers came into view. I crouched low, but one of them spotted me right off.

Uh-oh, busted! I thought. I'm not quite sure why I didn't run. Maybe it was the muskets they pointed at me.

Heading straight toward me was a large, red-haired gentleman. He carried his hat in his hand, using it to fan himself. The second man I guessed to be a lawyer because of his black clothing and white wig. Bringing up the rear was a man dressed as a sheriff's officer. The men drew close and dismounted. As I took a step back, they suddenly surrounded me like a pack of wolves.

"State yer business," ordered the red-haired man.

"To whom am I speaking?" I said, trying to sound brave.

"I am Colin Roy Campbell, a loyal subject of King George. Now, state yer business."

It was the Red Fox! I stood rigid. "I'm on my way to the home of James of the Glens."

As he tilted his head in thought, Red Fox said to the lawyer, "There's many a man who would think this a warning. Here I am on my way to rid the Highlands of those not loyal to our king, and suddenly a young lad"—

his hand motioned to me—"a kinsman of James, jumps out of the ferns at me."

"If ye are concerned about me," said I, "don't be. I am neither of his people nor yers. I am but an honest subject of King George." I wagged my tail to show my sincerity.

The Red Fox eyed me. "If that is true, what business brings ye so far from the Lowlands?"

"I—"A gunshot, fired from the hill above, split the air and cut off my words. Red Fox crumpled to the ground, clutching his bleeding chest. He released a jagged sigh, and then his head rolled to one side. I stared in horror. Red Fox was dead!

From the hill above, I saw movement. I pointed and called out, "The murderer!" I scrambled up the hillside.

Running among the trees, I caught a glimpse of the man. He was big, and he wore a black coat with metal buttons. In his hand he carried a long gun.

"Here!" I cried to the others below. "I see him!"

"Halt!" ordered the sheriff's man.

Slowing, I looked back. His command was meant for me! A troop of redcoats, muskets in hand, had joined him and the lawyer.

"But he's getting away!" I barked.

"A reward if ye take that lad!" cried the lawyer to the soldiers. "He's an accomplice. He was left here to distract us until the murderer arrived."

"Ye've got it all wrong!" My heart beat like a drum. Life was full of surprises, and they weren't all good. Not only had I been stripped of my rightful inheritance, but now I was being unjustly accused of participating in Red Fox's murder!

The soldiers began to fan out, some taking aim with their muskets to cover me. I froze.

"Duck in here!" whispered a voice from the trees. I

heard the guns fire as I jumped to safety. Then, turning, I faced the man who'd just saved me.

"Alan!" I couldn't believe it. But there he stood, with a fishing rod in one hand and a musket in the other. Not long ago he'd saved me from Hoseason and his crew. Now here he was, saving my hide again.

"Come," said he, dropping his rod.

We glanced at the soldiers, and then fled. We ran among the birch trees, stooped low behind rocks, and crawled on all fours among the heather bushes. Sometimes the bushes seemed soft, but most of the time they were coarse and stiff. I got scratched from my nose to my tail.

Going on all fours was easier for me than it was for Alan. But the pace was difficult for both of us. My heart seemed to be bursting against my ribs. Every now and then Alan would straighten himself to his full height and look back. And every time he did, there came a loud, faraway cheering from the soldiers.

It was as if Alan *wanted* to be seen! Would I ever make it to Rankeillor's alive?

Later, Alan stopped, lay flat on the ground, and turned to me, panting. "Now, do as I do to save your life."

At the same speed as before, but with more caution this time, we traced our way back across the mountainside the same way we had come. This time Alan didn't stand and show himself to any soldiers. Thank goodness! But I was puzzled. *What is going on?* I thought.

At last Alan threw himself down in the same woods where he'd called out to me in the trees after Red Fox's murder. His chest heaved as he struggled to catch his breath. Dog-tired myself, I dropped and joined him. Finally, we napped.

Alan was the first to stir. I said nothing but thought plenty. A man Alan hated had been murdered. And here was Alan, hiding in the trees and running from the troops. *Did he fire the fatal shot?* I wondered. *Or did he give the order?* Either way, he was linked to the murder. Though Alan had saved my life, I couldn't even look him in the eye.

"Are ye still wearied?" he asked, brushing heather flowers from his coat and breeches.

"We must separate," I said, my tail hanging low.

"What?" cried Alan, surprised.

"Alan," said I, "ye know very well the Campbell Red Fox is dead."

Alan took out his knife and laid his hand upon it. "I swear, David, that I had neither killed nor plotted to kill the Red Fox."

It was as if a crushing weight had been lifted from my furred shoulders. "Thank goodness for that!"

I did a half flip, which was the best I could do. I offered him my paw. He refused to shake it. I frowned.

"Ye can't blame me for my thoughts, Alan. Ye know

very well what ye told me on the ship." I offered him my paw again.

"I saw the man fleeing on the hillside, same as ye." He put on his hat. "But being a man on the run myself, I thought I'd do the fellow a favor and draw the soldiers away from him." He cocked his head. "Perhaps he's done my kinsmen a favor."

A favor? I thought. I couldn't think of murder as a favor.

Finally, Alan took my paw in both of his hands. "Surely ye have cast a spell on me, David. I could forgive ye anything." Then he grew serious. "We must flee, too. As word of the shooting spreads, everyone will believe I killed Red Fox. And ye have already been linked to his death. Troops will be searching all of Appin for us."

"But they're barking up the wrong tree. I'm innocent!" I howled.

"Hoot," said Alan. "It's a Campbell who's been killed. Ye'd be tried in Campbell territory, with fifteen Campbells in the jury box, and another one for yer judge."

I was beginning to see his point.

"Either go on the run with me, or else hang," said Alan.

"Okay, I'm convinced. I'll pass on wearing the rope collar. I don't want to hang." A shiver shook my body as I let the seriousness of our situation sink in. We were accused murderers on the run!

"We're in the Highlands, David, where King George's soldiers are trying to get rid of any rebels and sympathizers of Prince Charles. When I tell ye to run, take my word and run." He adjusted his knife sheath and his belt. He checked his musket. "We'll hide by day and travel by night . . . to the Lowlands."

Yes! Those last three words were music to my

floppy ears. I still had a bone to pick with my uncle, and I was anxious to get back to the land that was rightfully mine.

Looking out from among the trees, Alan and I could see a steep mountainside—more rough stone and heather bushes. From this distance we saw the soldiers as they went up and down the hills, growing smaller every moment. No doubt they thought we were closer.

"We still have a long way to go," said Alan. "We're only halfway to Queensferry."

Queensferry! Where my uncle had left me in the hands of my kidnapper, Captain Hoseason.

My paws were beginning to look like chewed-up leather, and we were only halfway there! "Are ye sure?" I asked. "It seems like months have passed since I was thrown from the ship and ye escaped from the sinking *Covenant*."

"Aye." Alan nodded. "But it's been closer to two weeks."

Sighing, I dropped and put my head on my paws. It would be another two weeks before I'd reach the house and see my uncle's lawyer.

As soon as the sun began to set, we started on our journey. Between sniffing the ground here and there, I told Alan of my adventures after being cast overboard.

"I had hoped that ye would get to land." He bent down and clapped a hand on my furred shoulder. "Ye bobbed up and down, up and down. Finally, I caught a glimpse of ye holding onto a piece of wood. I hoped ye had survived, so I left ye messages."

Hearing a rustle, I stopped, lifted my nose, and sniffed. Alan stopped, too. Then some night creature—perhaps a bat—landed in one of the bigger bushes. I didn't catch a scent of danger, so we continued on.

"What happened to the captain and the crew?" I asked.

"Those on deck jumped into the rowboat and we set to rowing. Before we were two hundred yards away, a great wave forced the ship clean over the reef and pushed her down." He sighed. "The men belowdecks never had a chance."

I shuddered.

"Upon reaching shore," said Alan, "Mr. Riach wanted to set me free, which caused quite a stir among the crew. I left the crew and the captain fighting one another."

We walked for hours, stumbling our way through the dark. I could see better in the dark than Alan, so I warned him of hazards whenever I could. At the top of a hill we saw light below us, coming from an open door. Beyond was torchlight. It seemed to be floating through the darkness like a firefly. Alan smiled, then whistled three times. Suddenly, the torch below came to a stop.

"Come," Alan said. "This is the house of my kinsman, James of the Glens. We will be welcome here."

I trotted after him obediently. When we reached the house, Alan introduced me to James but did not give away my name. Alan told him of the situation.

James pulled Alan aside to talk, but my keen hearing caught every single word. "They're searching the Appin region," said James, "looking for the murderer. I've a family to protect." He paused. "The two of ye cannot stay here. I advise ye both to change yer clothes before ye go, so ye're not recognized. I'll bury what ye're wearing."

"Bury my fine French clothes! No! No! I will take the risk!" cried Alan.

But I was ready to shed my flea-bitten rags for something clean. And I most definitely did not want to be recognized! I was glad I didn't have any special markings—like Alan and his pockmarked skin—that made me stand out in a crowd.

As we got ready to leave, James handed Alan a bag of oatmeal and a pan, a deerskin flask full of water, and then a sword. Alan exchanged his musket for a pistol. "They'll have a reward out for ye and yer friend's capture," James warned.

A price on our heads? As in . . . yikes! . . . dead or alive!?

Alan frowned. "Then it's a good thing nobody knows yer name," Alan said, pointing to me. He hooked the weapons and food to his belt, and then we headed eastward, up and out of the valley.

Sometimes we walked, sometimes we ran, passing huts and houses partially hidden in the hills. Whenever we heard a fern or a bush rustle, we froze in our tracks. It was always a rabbit or a deer, but we had to be careful. With a price on our heads, there was always the danger that even one of Alan's trusted friends might betray us for the money. They were so poor, who could blame them?

We stopped long enough for Alan to mix some water and oatmeal in the pan. I was surprised when he scooped up a handful of the uncooked porridge and ate.

"A man on the run can't have a fire to cook by." Alan nodded at the food. "Cold oatmeal has often filled my belly. Dig in, man."

I put my nose in the pan and sniffed. It wasn't stew, but hey, beggars can't be choosers. I lapped up my share. Then we continued on.

Somehow we stayed safe through the night. But the sun rose while we were in a big, wide valley. Talk about bad timing! Broad daylight, and the place was as flat as a pancake, with nowhere to hide!

Fear showed on Alan's face. "This is a place they're bound to watch. We can't stay here."

He broke into a hard run toward a river. I ran after him.

The rushing river was split into three sections by two boulders. Backing up to get a running start, Alan jumped to the first one. Without thinking, I followed right behind him.

The water thundered between the boulders; fear and vibration made my belly quake. Spray soaked my coat and face. One wrong move and I'd be swept away in the current. I stared at the next boulder. It was very far away.

My four paws seemed stuck to the slippery rock on which we stood. I was frozen with fear.

Water raged around us. Alan's mouth moved and I knew he was speaking. But I couldn't hear him over the thundering of the river, even though we were both on the same rock and standing close.

Putting his hands to his mouth, and his mouth to my spotted ear, he shouted, "Snap out of it, David! There's a price on our heads." He shook my shoulders. "To be afraid of a thing and yet do it is what makes the best kind of a man. Ye can do this!" He forced me to look into his eyes. "Will ye follow my lead? I can't lose ye, David."

Numbly, I nodded. With that, Alan leaped and reached the next boulder. He turned and coaxed me on.

I knew I had to follow or drown. Releasing a shiver, I crouched low on all fours and sprang. But my jump was too short. Everything below my big black spot plunged into the cold river. I clawed at the slippery boulder with my front paws, while the current pulled at my hind legs. I tried not to gulp water. Suddenly, I felt Alan's hands grab my collar.

"Come on, man, pull!"

As he yanked me to safety, his right foot slipped into the water, but he managed to keep himself from going in completely. I sighed. Once again Alan had saved my tail!

After taking a couple of quick breaths, we jumped the short distance to the opposite riverbank. Alan took off running again.

I gave myself a good shake. Looking around, I realized we were still out in the open. We were easy targets! I scampered off after Alan.

Hours passed before we found enough cover of bushes to stop and rest. I collapsed by Alan's side and waited till my breathing slowed. "Thank ye so much for not letting me drown."

Alan patted my furred shoulder. "What are friends for?"

I'd never known a man like Alan. He had no problem risking his own neck to save someone else's. Even a stranger's.

The last thing I heard before drifting off to sleep was the crying of eagles. No sooner had I started to dream than Alan clapped his hand around my muzzle and nudged me awake. A finger was to his lips. "The soldiers are coming!" he whispered urgently.

Crouching, we sneaked off through the bushes again. Up hills, down hills, across rocks . . . I was hungry and exhausted!

At nightfall, we hired someone with almost the last of our money to take us across the lake we'd come to. The man was slim and stooped, and as unfriendly as a cat. He reminded me of Ebenezer. My heartbeat quickened as I thought of seeing my uncle again. What would I do to even the score?

Jumping from the boat, we again ran through the darkness. Finally, Alan stopped. "We'll rest here."

Looking up, I saw why he'd stopped. A great rock rose some twenty feet high. Backing up to get a good run at it, Alan then tried to scramble up the side. It was not until his third attempt that he finally got enough momentum to make it up. I, with four paws, had it just a bit easier.

The top of the rock sloped inward, forming a saucerlike dish—a perfect place for two men to hide.

"At last!" I circled, lay down, and was about to put my head on my paws when I noticed Alan. He looked like a rag doll someone had dropped. The man was exhausted. Each time we stopped, he had been standing guard, while I rested.

Shaking myself awake, I sat up. "It's my watch, Alan. Ye need to rest."

He nodded. "Thank ye, David. Wake me soon and I'll let ye have a few winks." In two shakes of my tail, Alan was asleep.

The night air was cold now that we weren't on the move. Hunkering down to stay warm, I blinked. Every part of me ached—even my whiskers. I blinked again. It felt so good to relax. . . .

The next thing I knew, Alan's hand was around my muzzle, once again, and he was shaking me awake. His expression was both angry and fearful as he looked over the edge of our rock silently and pointed to the soldiers on horses fanning out around us. It was misty, but I could see them clearly. Too clearly. It was daylight!

My heart jumped into my throat. Shame burned through me like hot coals. I turned away. I'd give my right ear to change what had happened. I had fallen asleep on my watch. I had let Alan down! And now we could both die because of my error.

When we last left Joe, he was in trouble, as well.

Chapter Ten

It was almost dark, and Joe was out in the garage cleaning out the last few items. Ellen had offered to complete the job, but Joe refused. Finished, he brought his camping gear inside. Wishbone followed him up to his room.

Piling the stuff near the window seat, Joe stared at it. He began to pace.

"You're like a dog in a kennel, Joe."

"So what if Curtis wasn't the one to write 'Sale Canceled'?" he muttered. "He deserves to get in trouble for what he did to David and me. It wasn't easy getting our bikes home." Joe sighed, stopping for a moment to look out his window. "David's busy baby-sitting, and Sam is out of town. I need someone to talk to."

"Helllooo! I'm an excellent listener, Joe. But if you prefer, why don't you try Ellen? She's very fair-minded."

"Joe?" Ellen's voice shot up the stairs, startling Joe. "There's an old movie starting on television. Do you want to come down and watch it with me? I'm going to make some popcorn."

Wishbone leaped off the bed. "On my way, Ellen!"

"Uh . . . sure, Mom. Be right down," Joe called.

Wishbone padded down the stairs. "Coming, coming, coming, coming . . ." He waited for Joe. Then the two went into the kitchen.

Ellen looked over her shoulder at them and smiled as the kernels slowly began to pop. "I feel like having butter tonight. How about you?"

Joe shrugged. "I'm not very hungry."

A look of concern clouded Ellen's face. "You didn't eat much dinner. Is everything okay, Joe?"

"Yeah." He avoided looking at her and headed to the refrigerator. "Lemonade or iced tea?"

"Lemonade," Ellen said over the pop, pop-pop, pop of the popcorn.

Joe poured two glasses of lemonade and took them into the living room.

"I'm sure it's just an oversight," Wishbone said, sitting at Joe's feet, "but I'll have some nice fresh water, thank you."

"What channel, Mom?" Joe called, turning on the television set.

"Four." Ellen came in with the bowl of popcorn.

"The movie's called *Make Way for Montgomery*." She sat down on the sofa and popped a few kernels of corn into her mouth. "It's really funny. I won't tell you any more— I don't want to spoil it."

Wishbone sat up. "Look, everybody! It's the cute dog, begging. He likes popcorn, too."

The doorbell rang.

"Could somebody get that, please?" Wishbone held his begging pose. "Thanks, Joe," he said, when Joe got up. Wishbone perked up his ears and listened.

"Oh, hi, Miss Gilmore. Come in."

"Thanks, Joe." Wanda came in and collapsed tiredly in a chair. Her flower-print hat was slipping to one side of her head, and her clothes seemed rumpled. "What a night!"

"Wanda, are you all right?" Ellen asked.

"Oh, I think so, Ellen. The historical society got in so many donations that extra people had to be called in to help price things and set up for the big sale tomorrow." She perked up and tried to straighten her hat. "This should be a great money-maker for the society—as long as Curtis's stunt doesn't put a damper on things."

"Maybe it wasn't Curtis," Joe said, turning away. "I'll get you some lemonade, Miss Gilmore."

"Thank you, Joe."

"Remember, water for me, Joe," Wishbone called, dropping down from his begging pose. "No ice."

Wanda took the glass Joe brought her and looked at the TV screen. "It's *Make Way for Montgomery!*" she said excitedly. "I love this old movie. This guy, Montgomery, tells a ton of lies." Her glance still glued to the TV, she got up and moved to the sofa to sit with Ellen. She took a handful of popcorn. "My favorite part is the end—you know, when Montgomery is trying to remember who he told what lie to. He gets so confused it's hilarious." She patted the sofa cushion. "Come on, Joe. Sit down."

Ellen cast him an apologetic look.

"I think I'll go up to my room, instead."

"What! No popcorn?" Wishbone followed Joe as he trudged up the stairs. "How about a doggie bag, Joe?"

Joe flopped onto his bed and stared at the ceiling.

Wishbone jumped up beside him. After awhile he closed his eyes. Just as Wishbone was drifting off to sleep, Joe bolted off the bed.

"I wish I'd never seen Curtis at the park today! Or I wish someone else had seen him there, too!" He began to pace. "Even when he's not trying to make my life miserable, he still manages to do it."

"I know, Joe." Wishbone sighed softly.

Joe looked out the window, then paced some more. "And it would serve Curtis right to take the blame for what happened at the *Chronicle*. He's been nothing but trouble."

Finally, Joe grabbed his backpack, unzipped it, and dug through it.

"Guess I'll play some solitaire," he said, pulling out his deck of cards.

Wishbone watched for a long time as Joe played silently. "Let's see," Wishbone said. "You lay the cards down, move them around, then pick them up. Then you mix the cards up and start again. No chewing, no tossing, no burying." He wagged his tail. "I don't get it."

Joe checked his watch and put away the cards. He lay back on the bed, on his side, next to Wishbone. Propping his head on one hand, he stroked Wishbone's back with the other.

"That's the spot, Joe. If you keep stroking it, we'll both feel better."

Joe glanced at his watch again. "This has been one of the longest days of my life."

Joe is really in a tight spot. And so are David Balfour and Alan Breck. Will they be able to make a run for it? Or will they be captured and sent to the gallows?

Chapter Eleven

Keeping low, I peered over the rim of the boulder, where I had fallen asleep when I was on watch. Below, the soldiers who had spread out around us drew closer. They had not discovered us.

"What do we do now?" I asked Alan, my tail drooping in shame because I'd slept on the job.

"We'll have to take our chances and cross through the line of soldiers," he snapped.

"What!" The fur on my neck bristled.

Alan scowled and whispered, "We have no choice! If we are driven back to Appin, we are two dead men!" He breathed deeply, trying to control his anger. "Do ye see that mountain yonder?" He pointed to a peak rising up into the northeastern sky. "It's full of hills and hollows, but few people. We'll head for it at the first chance."

We lay damp and shivering in the hollow of the boulder. Soon the pockets of mist disappeared and the sun warmed my fur. "Feels good to the bone, doesn't it, Alan?" I whispered, rolling to let the sun warm the fur on my side. But Alan didn't answer me. *Okay, be that way*, I thought, rolling over again.

I heard the neigh of horses as some of the soldiers rode ahead. I peeked out. Alan yanked me back down, but not before I saw that at least half the soldiers were still nearby.

As the morning wore on and the sun rose higher, the rock itself grew warmer. I began to pant. Before long, Alan and I were both very uncomfortable. The hot sun turned the rock underneath us into a fiery griddle. Alan and I shared what little water we had left. Water had been so plentiful in our travels that we took time to refill the flask only when it was almost empty.

Alan glanced over the rim of the boulder. His cheeks were as red as the coats on the soldiers. Sweat ran down his face in streams. "Get ready to go—or we'll fry up here like fish." Alan looked out twice more.

"They are not looking in our direction. Now, David, be quick!" On his stomach, he slid feet first over the side and hung onto the rim of the boulder. He struggled to find footholds on the rock. When he found one, he searched for another. Slowly, he worked his way downward. I watched in horror, my heart pounding. How would I get down? I heard a noise and gazed out off the opposite side of the boulder. The soldiers seemed to be looking away. It was now or never for me.

Crouching low, I looked for the footholds in the boulder that Alan had used. Instead of going straight down, I belly-crawled, zigging and zagging from one small ledge to another. It seemed like the soldiers' voices were nearer now, but it was hard to tell with the blood pounding in my ears. I saw Alan jump to the ground.

Alan scampered up the hill on his hands and knees, incredibly fast, as if it were his natural way of moving. He headed for the cover of the heather bushes.

Just before I was going to jump from the boulder,

my front paws slipped. I fell to the ground. A whimper escaped my lips as I rolled.

Shouts rose from the soldiers. I could only assume they had heard me.

I stood. I felt bruised but not seriously hurt. After glancing over my tail and seeing no one, I quickly followed Alan.

We wove in and out of the heather bushes. Some of them had been blackened by fire. A blinding, choking dust rose in our faces and made it hard to breathe. Still, I could always smell soldiers and horses not far away. It was as if they were everywhere, yet not directly on our tail.

We kept going, stopping to lie down and rest only when we found a big enough bush for cover.

At the coming of night, we found ourselves near the beginning of the mountain range. Hearing a trumpet sound, we stopped behind the shelter of a bush and watched the soldiers, who were searching for us, gather. It was a small group of men. They began to build a fire to camp for the night.

"At last, we can sleep!" Just as I was about to curl up and tuck my tail against my side, Alan bent over me.

"There shall be no sleep tonight!" He nudged me to my feet. "We got through just in time, and now we'll continue on."

"Please!" I begged. "I'm dog-tired!"

Alan glared. "There are worse things than being tired, David. One is death."

I could tell by his voice he was still angry with me for falling asleep on my watch. "I ache from my fall and I don't have the strength to go on," I said. "I would, but as sure as I'm alive, I cannot."

"Very well," said Alan stiffly. "I'll carry ye." Bending

111

down, he placed his hands under my belly and lifted me to his chest.

His determination to keep us alive shamed me. "Wait." I drew strength from him and jumped from his arms. "Lead on. I'll follow."

We set off again. It grew cooler. Heavy mist fell and drenched us like rain. Shivering, I kept going, stumbling forward. Alan was in the right career as a soldier. It was an officer's job to make his men push themselves, and he made me push on.

Finally, we came to the ridge of a mountain, the one that Alan had pointed out to me from the distant, saucer-like boulder. Safety at last! As we half-ran, half-stumbled across a heather-covered hillside, my keen hearing alerted me to a rustle. I tried to reach out with my paw and touch Alan to warn him silently. But before I could, four ragged men leaped out of the bushes and threw us to the ground. The next moment Alan and I were on our backs, with knives at our throats. The men standing over us were sun-darkened and filthy.

Of course, *my* clothes and fur probably didn't look so great by then, either! I didn't move a whisker. But my heart pounded from fear as I felt the cold point of the knife against my throat. Would these men kill us right then? Or would they send us to the gallows so they could claim the reward money?

Alan talked in Gaelic. The men drew back and looked at us strangely, but they put their knives away.

Alan smiled. "We couldn't have fallen into better hands; they're on our side—rebel supporters." He put a reassuring hand on my furred shoulder. "We'll spend the night here, with them—they'll help us keep watch for King George's soldiers."

"Nap time! Now, that's a language I understand." I

dropped to my belly and used my paws as a pillow. "Good night, Alan." The last thing I remembered was a man bringing out playing cards and dealing to Alan and the others.

In the morning, I awoke to find the men gone. Alan stood, staring out across the land. He held his hat in his hands and had a guilty look about him.

"Forgive me, David. While ye were sleeping soundly, I borrowed coins from yer purse. I lost what little money we had by betting on the cards."

"What?" I barked, jumping up to all fours.

Alan stood quite still, the tails of his great coat flapping behind him in the wind. "I'm sorry, David."

I started to growl. Then I remembered my own mistake, which had almost cost us our lives. I patted my purse with my paw. I held a few coins, along with Alan's button, pressed against my chest. Alan's mistake was not nearly as serious as mine. I stepped closer to him. "I forgive ye, Alan. Can ye forgive me for falling asleep on watch?"

"I already have, David." Alan offered his hand and shook my paw. "Now ye need to forgive yourself."

We continued our travels, moving mostly by night. Our stomachs growled more often than not, but somehow the oatmeal had lasted, and we managed to find berries and plants to eat. Still, I would have cut off my right whiskers for a decent bowl of kibble.

It was in July when we finally made our way to the region of the Lowlands. More than one month ago, the *Covenant* had sailed with me as a prisoner.

"Surely the hunt for us has slowed with the passing of time," I said.

"Ye're in your own land again." Alan smiled. "From here on, ye should be safe, David. Since yer name was never mentioned, no one will link ye to the murder. I'll be returning to France once we reach Queensferry."

I flipped in the air as I thought about finally meeting with my uncle's lawyer. "Rankeillor, here I come!" Then my tail drooped as my thoughts turned to Alan. He wouldn't be safe until he reached France. Was that even possible?

The worry stayed with me all the way to Queensferry, where just outside of town my uncle lived.

"I can't believe we finally made it to Queensferry," I said, eyeing the place. My tail went into a high-speed wag. The stars seemed brighter and the air sweeter than on any other night in my life. The following morning I'd be scratching at the lawyer's door, ready to claim my inheritance. I barked with joy. "Good-bye, Ebenezer!"

"Quiet," Alan reminded me, crouching. "I'll not be welcomed here with open arms."

"Sorry," I said.

That night I hardly slept. It wasn't because of sore paws, my four aching legs, or even hunger. As eager as I was to see the lawyer Rankeillor, I had no proof of my rights or of my identity. My only proof, the letter from my father, was in the hands of my uncle!

The next day Alan and I made plans. We agreed he'd stay hidden in the hills while I went to the lawyer's. Then at sunset Alan would wait by the roadside until he heard me whistle a special tune.

"Good luck to ye, David."

Nodding, I trotted on to town. Then I asked for directions to the lawyer's home.

Flowerpots lined the steps leading to his front door. I stopped to sniff each one. Nice, I thought, but not much room for digging. The house itself had beautiful clear-glass windows—perfect for making nose prints.

Dirty from muzzle to tail, and with only three coins left in my purse, I knocked on Mr. Rankeillor's door.

A ruddy-faced man wearing spectacles and a well-powdered wig answered the door. He looked me over, then frowned.

"Please don't turn me away because of my looks." I held my tail high. "My name is David Balfour."

"David Balfour?" he repeated, in a rather doubtful tone. "Well . . . come in."

He led me into a dusty room full of books and dog-eared documents. Sitting, he pulled out some papers. "Sit," he commanded, pointing to a chair across from his desk.

I jumped up into the chair and sat down. I looked Mr. Rankeillor in the eye. "I have reason to believe I have rights to the Shaws estate."

The lawyer shifted in his chair. "Come, come, Mr. Balfour. You must continue. Where were you born? Who

were your father and your mother? Have you any papers proving your identity? Speak up."

I answered his questions and explained everything—the letter, the kidnapping, and the shipwreck.

"You say you were shipwrecked," said the lawyer, rubbing his forehead. "Where was that?"

"Off the south tip of the Isle of Mull. I swam to the island of Earraid."

Mr. Rankeillor nodded. "So far, what you say agrees with my other information." He looked at his papers. "But the *Covenant* was lost on June 17. Today is July 24." He raised a brow. "Where have you been all this time?"

I wagged my tail slowly. "How can I be sure I'm talking to a friend? I was shipped off by the very man who ye work for."

A smile crossed his face. "I was indeed your uncle's lawyer. But while you have been away, a good deal has happened."

Mr. Rankeillor drew in a deep breath before he went on to explain.

"On the very day of your sea disaster, the minister of Essendean, Mr. Campbell, walked into my office and demanded to see you."

I smiled as I thought of my father's friend, kindly Mr. Campbell.

Mr. Rankeillor continued. "Well, I'd never heard of your existence, but I'd known your father." Mr. Rankeillor shifted in his chair. "I called upon Ebenezer. He said he'd given you considerable sums of money and that you had started out for Europe. Ebenezer also said that you had expressed a desire to break with your past life. And he claimed to know nothing of your whereabouts."

"He's a liar and a sneak!" I leaped to my paws.

Mr. Rankeillor rummaged through the papers on his

desk until he found a blank sheet. "I didn't believe him, but I had no proof. Then word came from Captain Hoseason. With the story of your drowning, your uncle's words proved false. It was another blot upon your uncle's character—one he could not afford." He pushed his spectacles up on his nose. "Now, do you think you can trust me?"

"Yes," I said. "But if I tell ye my story, I'll put a friend's life in yer hands. Promise me he'll be kept safe."

"I give you my word as long as you mention no names." Pushing his glasses up to his forehead, Mr. Rankeillor leaned back, closed his eyes, and told me to begin.

I was afraid he'd fall asleep. But he heard every word I said about my life on the run. I got so caught up in telling my story that I slipped and mentioned the name "Alan Breck."

Instantly, the lawyer sat up and opened his eyes wide. Of course! By that time, Alan's name had rung through Scotland with the news of the murder of Red Fox in the north.

"Name no unnecessary names, Mr. Balfour!" Mr. Rankeillor warned. Leaning back in his chair, he again closed his eyes. "I have dull hearing, so I didn't catch the name correctly. From this point on, we will call your friend 'Mr. Thomson.'"

"Yes, sir," I said obediently, wishing the cat had gotten my tongue a moment ago. From then on I was careful. Throughout the rest of my story, Alan was "Mr. Thomson."

"Well, well." The lawyer straightened and looked at me when I was done. "You have wandered far. And this Mr. Thomson seems to me to be a gentleman of some choice qualities, though perhaps a little bloody-minded."

I nodded.

"And I suppose in your wanderings you have had plenty of time to wonder why your father and your uncle lived like strangers."

"Yes." I wagged my tail anxiously.

"Well, the two lads fell in love with the same lady," he said flatly. "Your mother."

I gasped. "Did my mother . . ." The thought was so horrible that the words caught in my throat. "Did she ever love Ebenezer?" I blurted out.

"Your uncle wasn't always old and quarrelsome." Waving his hand, Rankeillor dismissed my question. "But he was as greedy then as he is now, and your father knew it. So after a long quarrel, the two struck a bargain. One man took the lady, the other the estate."

Unbelievable! Uncle Ebenezer had traded love and happiness for wealth. No wonder he became such an evil, bitter man.

Mr. Rankeillor straightened the papers on his desk. "The estate is yours beyond a doubt. By law, you are the heir. It matters not at all what your father signed when he was a lad." He stroked his chin. "But your uncle is a man who would put up a fight. He might call your identity into question." His eyebrows shot up. "A lawsuit is expensive. Besides, your adventures with Mr. Thomson might be made public." He shook his head. "We need some way to prove the kidnapping out of court."

I jumped down from the chair and paced for a while. "Well, sir," I said, sitting by his feet, "after chewing on some ideas, a plan has finally come to mind." With that, I discussed my plot with him.

Chapter Twelve

I put my nose to the floor and looked around Mr. Rankeillor's office while he wrote up the paper needed for my plan. Not a crumb of food to be had! At last he rang a bell and his clerk came into the room.

"Torrance," he said, "write this up immediately as a legal document. Then, when you've finished that, will you be so kind as to put on your coat and hat? You're needed to come along as a witness."

"Yes, sir." Torrance nodded, then excused himself.

Mr. Rankeillor poured himself a glass of wine. "The very sight of Torrance reminds me of a story of some years ago." He smiled. "Torrance and I had set off together, then split up to do errands. When the time came to meet up again, I couldn't find my spectacles. I was so blind without them that I did not recognize my own clerk!" He laughed heartily.

I smiled out of politeness, but the story wasn't that funny. And he repeated it!

Finally, Torrance returned with his coat and hat, and a basket hung from his arm.

I sniffed. I smelled food. My nose led me right to Torrance's basket. A doggie bag!

The three of us set off. I trotted beside the other two, stopping occasionally to sniff around. All through town Mr. Rankeillor said hello to people we passed. He knew just about everybody.

At last we were clear of the houses, near the inn at Queensferry. Being there again, remembering what had happened on the *Covenant*, I shuddered from nose to tail. Suddenly the lawyer cried out, causing the fur on my neck to bristle. He ran his hands over his pockets, then began to laugh.

"Why," he said, "if this doesn't beat all. After all that I said today, I have forgotten my glasses!"

Now I understood why he had repeated the story about his poor eyesight. With his glasses at home, Mr. Rankeillor could not, in a court of law, identify my friend. Clever!

"I'll go up ahead and scout around," I said, trotting off as I picked up Alan's scent. I went up the hill, whistling.

Finally, Alan rose from behind a bush. "It's good to see ye, David. Ye're early." He brushed the dirt and leaves from his breeches.

I wagged my tail, stood on my hind legs, and put my front paws on Alan's leg. "I have a plan to get my inheritance, but I need your help." I quickly explained everything. "Can I count on ye?"

"It's a good plan indeed," said Alan. "But I think yer lawyer friend might send me to the gallows."

"No, no. He thinks yer name is Thomson, and he forgot his glasses, so he can't identify ye."

When Alan nodded his approval, I motioned to Mr. Rankeillor and Torrance. "Hello—up here." Then I went on to introduce everyone. After that, we set out for my uncle's house—or, should I say, mine?

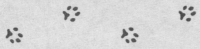

It was past ten when we reached the house. My nose twitched. The night was clear and mild, with a rustling breeze that covered the sound of our footsteps. The house was dark, and I assumed my uncle was in bed. We whispered the last of our plans. Then Mr. Rankeillor, Torrance, and I crept over and hid beside a corner of the house. I flattened my belly to the soft ground. Nosing out, I watched as Alan strode to the door and knocked.

He knocked louder and longer. Finally, an upstairs window was thrust open.

"What brings ye here this time of night?" cried my uncle angrily. "I have a gun!" He hoisted it in the air.

"What brings me here is more yer affair than mine. Are ye Ebenezer Balfour?" asked Alan.

"I am. What business is it of yers? And who might ye be?"

Alan smiled. "My name is of no concern to ye. But what brings me here is another story. I have news of David Balfour."

My uncle stiffened. "I'll be right down," he said in a changed voice.

The window slammed shut. A moment later I heard Ebenezer slide open every bolt and bar on the door. Then it creaked open and my uncle stepped out.

"I brought my gun. If ye take a step nearer, ye're good as dead."

"I'll get straight to the point," Alan said, removing his hat. "I have friends living near the Isle of Mull. It seems there was a ship lost in those parts. The next day, while my friends were seeking wood from the wrecked ship for their fires, they found a half-drowned lad." Alan

clicked his tongue. "Well, my friends revived him and brought him to an old castle. Aye. He's been a great expense, and my friends aren't well off."

Suddenly a flea bit my back, near my big black spot. I dared not dig at it, or else Ebenezer might spot me. Oh! It was difficult to sit still! I made myself focus on Alan's words.

"Finding out that the lad was yer natural-born nephew, Mr. Balfour, was good news to my friends. They asked me to call on ye and discuss the matter." He ran his fingers along the brim of his hat. "My friends are a bit wild, and not so particular about the law. I'll tell ye right off, unless we can agree upon some terms, ye are not likely to set eyes on David Balfour again."

My uncle cleared his throat. "I'm not very caring. He wasn't a good lad. I've no reason to interfere."

Not very caring? Try "grouchy," "heartless," and "cruel," I thought. *This guy doesn't have one kind bone in his entire body!*

"Aye, aye," said Alan, stroking his chin slowly. "I see what ye are doing—pretending ye don't care, to make the ransom smaller. Ye can't fool me, old man."

"Nah!" said Ebenezer, shaking his head firmly. "It's the truth. I take no interest in the lad." He scowled. "I'll pay no ransom, large or small!"

"Hoot!" said Alan. "Blood is thicker than water. Ye cannot desert yer brother's son for the shame it would bring ye." He nodded across the land. "Ye would not be very popular in your countryside."

"I'm not very popular the way it is," replied Ebenezer. "And if it came to that, I don't see how the word would get out. Not by me, and not by yer wild friends."

"Then it'll have to be David who tells it," said Alan.

"How's that?" said my uncle sharply.

"It can be only one of two ways. Either ye liked David and would pay to get him back . . ."—Alan paused and grinned slyly—". . . or else ye have good reasons for not wanting him back. It seems it's not the first option. Well, then, the second option should put money in my pocket and the pockets of my friends."

Ebenezer grumbled. "I don't follow ye."

"No?" Alan cocked his head. "If ye don't want the lad back, what do ye want done with him, and how much will ye pay?"

Ebenezer shuffled his feet uneasily.

"Well, sir?" cried Alan. "I need an answer, or I'll have to ram my sword through yer belly."

"Give me a minute," snarled my uncle. "And belly, say ye! Remember my gun?" He brought it up to his chest.

Alan leaned over him. "Before yer quivering finger could find the trigger, my sword would be in yer chest. Now, do ye want David killed, or kept?"

"Oh, sir, that's no way to talk!" Ebenezer looked flustered. "We'll have no bloodshed. I'm a man of honor. And besides, ye forget something—the lad is my brother's son."

"Aye," said Alan, rubbing his chin again. "Now, we must agree upon a sum. I want more than what ye paid Hoseason."

"Paid him for what?" cried my uncle.

"Kidnapping David."

My uncle gasped, as if he'd sucked down a bone. "He wasn't kidnapped!"

Alan moved a hand near his sword. "Don't lie to me, ye old runt! Hoseason and I are partners, and he told me everything."

"Truth is," my uncle confessed, watching Alan's hand, "I gave Hoseason twenty coins. He was to sell the lad in the Colonies in Caroliny and make more. But not from my pocket!"

At this, Mr. Rankeillor and Torrance stepped out of hiding.

"Thank ye, Mr. Thomson," said the lawyer. "I have all the information I need. My clerk, Torrance, here, is a witness."

I leaped out after them, prepared to growl at my uncle. But the sight of his sagging shoulders stopped me. He stared into the night like a man turned to stone. Alan took away his gun and we all went into the house. While Mr. Rankeillor and Ebenezer began to work out a deal at the kitchen table, Alan and I built up the fire.

Soon Rankeillor called me over. "I suggest that Ebenezer get one-third of the yearly income from the estate."

I looked at my uncle, old and pitiful. Close to two months earlier, as I lay in the hold of the *Covenant*, I would have denied him a bowl of water. But from Alan I'd learned firsthand about loyalty to kin. I nodded. "As the new landowner, that suits me fine."

Torrance opened up his basket of food and we all celebrated, except for my uncle. He took his food and slunk away like a cat to his bedroom.

I sat tall. I was now legally David Balfour of the house of Shaws! And I would do my best to bring honor back to my family name.

But later, when I was alone with Alan, a terrible thought occurred to me. My heart felt heavy as I went and sat by Alan. "If it weren't for me, ye'd be safely back in France by now."

"Aye, but where would ye be?" asked Alan, trying to

make light of his situation. "If not dead by yer shipmates' hands, then surely from the weather or starvation."

"Ye're right," I said.

"Then are ye glad, David?" he asked.

"I'm very grateful." But my heart felt heavier still, so heavy that if I were in water I would surely sink. Scotland meant death for Alan—the Highlands were filled with King George's soldiers searching everywhere for rebels, and the Lowlands were filled with the king's followers. Had Alan sacrificed his life for mine?

David Balfour has finally come home.

Now let's bark up another tree and see what Joe is going to do. Will he continue to hide the truth so he can camp out in Jackson Park? Or will he be spending the night at home?

Chapter Thirteen

The next afternoon David showed up at the Talbots' door and rang the doorbell. Joe opened the door. David smiled and pointed to the porch. "I have a lot of stuff to carry to the park. I thought maybe we could take some of it over before dinner."

"Sure," Joe said. "But first let's go upstairs and get my stuff."

Wishbone trotted up the stairs behind Joe and David. "Excuse me. Dog coming through." He pushed his way between the boys and went into Joe's room.

Joe walked to the window seat and scooped up his stuff. He glanced around. "Oh, and the radio." He looked around again. His glance stopped at his bed. "My pillow!" Balancing his load, he reached under the covers and grabbed it. "Anything else?"

Wishbone wagged his tail. "How about a blanket for the dog?"

David surveyed the room. "I don't think so, Joe. But we still have to get the soft drinks from the fridge." He turned on his heel. "Ready?"

"Helllooo! A blanket for the dog, remember? Would

somebody mind listening to the dog?" Wishbone followed the boys out of the room and trotted down the stairs after them.

"There you are!" Wanda said, coming down the hall with Ellen. With one hand she adjusted the chef's hat on her head; with the other hand, she carried a plate of cookies covered with plastic wrap. "I was baking cookies to sell at the rummage sale, so I whipped these up especially for you guys." She smiled proudly. "I know how much you like pizza, so I came up with my very own creation—pizza cookies!" She beamed. "I haven't tasted them yet, but I know they'll be good. The secret is lots of pepperoni. I even made one in the shape of a bone for Wishbone." She held out the plate. "See?"

Wishbone wagged his tail as he stretched for a better look. "I'm touched, Wanda. A bit surprised, but touched."

"Thanks, Miss Gilmore." Joe stuffed his pillow under his arm so he could take the plate.

"Yes, thanks." David smiled at her, then exchanged an eyebrow-raising glance with Joe.

Wishbone sniffed the air. "Loosen up, guys. I bet they're good. Crisp as week-old pizza crust!"

Wanda wiggled her fingers. "Maybe you could save one to give to Sam. Shouldn't she get back soon from her trip?"

"Well, I certainly hope so!" Wishbone said eagerly. "I really miss her behind-the-ear scratches."

"Sure." The boys nodded.

"Oh!" Wanda's eyes opened wide. "I almost forgot. My friend Marge just called to find out if I was going to be on the clean-up squad. Guess what she told me? She just talked to Officer Krulla, and he's on his way over to Curtis's house to speak to him."

Wishbone heard Joe sigh.

Joe looked at Ellen. "Mom, Miss Gilmore, I have to tell you something."

He handed the cookies back to Wanda, who wore the same surprised look on her face that Ellen did. Then he took a deep breath and unloaded his arms.

"Curtis didn't write on the *Chronicle* windows. He was at the park when that happened. I know, because I saw him there."

"That's my boy!" Wishbone barked.

Ellen looked even more surprised. "But, Joe, I thought I made it very clear that you were to stay home."

"You did, Mom," he said. "I'm sorry. I shouldn't have left the house. Before we talk about it, can I go over to Curtis's and get him off the hook?"

"Of course," Ellen said.

David nodded. "I'll go with you."

Wanda looked around for a place to set down the cookies. "We'll all go!"

They all hopped into Ellen's car and were at Curtis's house in a few minutes.

"Hurry, guys!" Jumping out of the car, Wishbone was the first to arrive in Curtis's yard. "Before they send an innocent kid to the pound for life!"

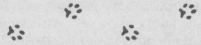

Officer Krulla stood on the front steps talking with Curtis. His father stood by, scowling.

"I didn't do it," Curtis said. "Honest! I was at the park this afternoon."

Running across the yard, Joe overheard Curtis's remark and stopped at the steps. He took a deep breath. "I saw him at the park, Officer Krulla."

Curtis shot Joe a worried look as Wanda, Ellen, and David caught up.

Wishbone cocked his head. "Hmm . . . That's an odd look to give someone to show your thanks."

Joe looked confused. "Yesterday afternoon while I was in Jackson Park, I saw Curtis. He was on the tire swing, wri——."

"Well, you're innocent this time," Curtis's dad said, interrupting Joe.

"You're sure about this?" Officer Krulla began to scribble in his notebook.

"Yes, sir," Joe said.

Curtis's dad looked relieved.

Wishbone heard a *whoosh!*, looked up, and saw a bike speeding toward them. "Incoming!" He jumped onto the steps as the bike skidded to a stop next to Joe. Wishbone groaned.

Straddling his bike and rolling it back and forth, Damont grinned. "What's going on?"

"Someone scrawled on several of the windows at the *Chronicle* with white paint," Wanda said. "Curtis was a suspect. Joe, here, was explaining to Officer Krulla that Curtis didn't do it."

Looking at Wanda, Damont suggested, "I bet whoever did it used something washable like shoe polish." Then he turned to Joe and said, "So, Mr. Nice Guy, just how do you know Curtis didn't do it?"

"I saw him in the park," Joe said. "He—"

Wishbone watched Curtis throw Joe a pleading look. Joe stopped abruptly. For some reason, Curtis didn't want anyone to know about the letter he was writing to his dad.

Joe looked back at Damont. "I saw him, that's all."

Officer Krulla turned his head and looked at Damont. "How do you know so much about shoe polish on windows?" he asked suspiciously.

"Yeah!" Wishbone sniffed Damont's bike tires. "Hmmm . . . Good dirt. In a pinch, I could pretend these are trees."

Damont glanced at Officer Krulla and fidgeted. "With school starting next week, several high-school

clubs have been writing notices on store windows with shoe polish to advertise their groups."

Officer Krulla eyed him, then put away his notebook and pencil. "Well, I guess that's it for here. I don't know if we'll ever catch the guilty party. Thank you for your cooperation. Have a nice day, everyone."

"'Bye," Wishbone replied, along with the others. As Wishbone fell into step with his people and got ready to head home, Curtis ran up to the group. He pulled Joe aside.

Wishbone perked up his ears and listened intently.

"Thanks, Talbot, for saving me—oh . . . and for not telling anybody what I was doing in the park," Curtis said.

"I don't understand why you don't want anyone to know," Joe said. "Weren't you just writing a letter to your dad?"

Resting his weight on one foot, Curtis crossed his arms over his chest. "It's a letter for his birthday—but it might ruin my image, Talbot, that's all."

Joe nodded. Then he caught up with David and the others.

Wishbone stepped in beside him.

"Now, about camping, Joe," Ellen said. "I think we need to discuss it when we get home."

The boys exchanged doubtful looks.

Joe nodded. "I know."

"Don't worry, Joe. Ellen's a fair person. Uh . . . but if it turns out we have to spend the night at home, do we still get to eat Wanda's cookies?"

Joe's camping adventure might be in trouble. But what about Alan? Will his adventure continue and take him safely to France, or will he be caught in Queensferry?

Chapter Fourteen

The next morning, before Mr. Rankeillor left the Shaws estate, we spoke privately. Grabbing a stick of wood in my teeth, I tossed it into the fire. "I must help my friend get out of the country, whatever the risk. But I'm not sure how."

"You seem to be in a difficult situation," he said. "If you get me a piece of paper, I think I can be of help."

"I'll see what I can dig up." Sniffing around, I found some sheets of blank paper in the reading room off the kitchen. I took one to him.

Sitting at the table, Mr. Rankeillor began to write. "This is a letter to my bankers, the British Linen Company," he explained. "I'm placing money in your name." He handed me the letter. "Mr. David, speak to your friend, Mr. Thomson. He will know of ways to leave the country. This money will help with the costs of his travel."

I put the letter safely in my pocket. "Thank ye, sir."

The lawyer nodded. "Good luck, Mr. David!" He stood, shook my paw, and then he and Torrance left.

I trotted across the hall to find Alan sitting in the

133

next room. His hat was in his lap, and he was gently smoothing its feather into shape.

"I've found a way to help you!"

Jumping up beside Alan, I told him about the bank credit. Together we decided that he should keep to the countryside, staying here, staying there. Mostly staying hidden. Meanwhile, I was to seek out a lawyer—one from the Appin region. Only an Appin Stewart could be wholly trusted! It would be his job to find a ship and arrange for Alan to board safely. When all the arrangements were made, the lawyer would send a messenger to Alan with the information.

"I have great faith in ye, David," Alan said, rising to his feet. He put on his hat and the two of us stepped out into the sunshine. I decided to walk Alan to Edinburgh, so we headed in that direction. My thoughts went to the silver button in my pocket. I didn't know whether to be sad or to flip for joy. I wanted Alan to be safe, but I didn't want him to go. We walked side by side in silence. I knew he felt the same way I did.

The farther we traveled, the heavier my heart felt.

I forced myself to sound happy. "I know!" I teased. "You could come live with me on my estate. You could get some un-French-like clothes and be 'Mr. Thomson' forever."

Alan forced a laugh. "Give up my French clothing? No!" He bent down and patted my shoulder. "That would never do."

We chuckled. Then the silence surrounded us again like a thick, dark cloud. I took a deep breath. In this past month, Alan Breck Stewart—a Highlander and an enemy of King George—had become the family I'd lost. But now he was leaving me, too.

Finally, just above Edinburgh, we reached a spot

called Rest-and-Be-Thankful. We stopped and looked over at the castle, then down at the city. Alan pointed out the spot where he would wait for the messenger, and we discussed when the man would come.

"Well, good-bye." Alan bent over and held out his hand.

"Good-bye," I said, and extended my paw to him.

Then suddenly Alan reached down and hugged me in his arms. "I love ye like a brother, David." Abruptly, he let go of me, turned away, and started down the hill. He did not look back.

I watched him until he was out of sight. Then I let out a great howl. I didn't know if I would ever see Alan Breck again. I did know I'd never forget him.

Chapter Fifteen

Ellen, Wanda, David, Joe, and Wishbone filed into the Talbots' living room. Joe sat down on the couch. Wishbone jumped up beside him.

"Oh! Wanda's cookies, right on the coffee table!" Wishbone stretched his neck toward them.

"No, Wishbone." David, sitting on his right, reached an arm out and gently nudged him back.

Wishbone sat down. "Why, David, I thought we were friends!"

Sitting in the chair next to Joe, Ellen only looked at him. When she finally spoke, her voice was calm. "You made a wrong choice this afternoon, Joe, when you left the house."

"I know, Mom. I'm sorry. I guess I was thinking too much about camping."

"You're right." She opened her mouth again to speak, but hesitated.

Joe stood. "I'll put my stuff away."

"I'll help you," David said, pushing himself up.

"Wait a minute." Ellen touched Joe's hand. "I'm not finished."

"Uh-oh, Joe." Wishbone put a paw over his eye. "It's worse than I thought."

Ellen tilted her head. "You also made a very good choice when you told the truth."

Joe's eyebrows shot up.

Coming to stand beside him, Wanda said, "You did the right thing. You saved Curtis at your own expense."

Wishbone looked proudly at Joe. "Let's celebrate. Pass the cookies!"

Ellen rested her hands on her legs. "And even though you left the house, you did have just about everything sorted for the rummage sale." She thought for a minute. "You can go ahead with your camping plans."

"I knew all along you were a fair person, Ellen," Wishbone said.

"Thanks, Mom." Joe looked at David and grinned. "Ready to go—"

The phone rang. Joe picked it up. "Hello? . . . Yes, she is. . . ." Looking, he began to smile. "Thank you. I'll tell her. 'Bye." He hung up. "Miss Gilmore, that was your friend Marge Martin. She's downtown and wanted you to know that the windows at the *Chronicle* have been washed and are free of graffiti. She also said someone posted a few more 'rummage sale' signs around town."

Wanda's hand went to her chest. "I'm thrilled the windows could be cleaned so easily. I guess Damont was right about the shoe polish. I feel badly about jumping to conclusions about Curtis."

"I wonder what else Damont knew," Wishbone said, as he joined Joe and David while they made their final preparations to camp out.

"Last one there's a rotten cat!" Wishbone took off out the door and headed in the direction of Jackson Park. When he didn't hear running footsteps alongside his own, he stopped and turned around.

David and Joe were heading toward the park. They were carrying their stuff, walking slowly and talking.

"Didn't you guys hear me?" Wishbone wagged his tail, ran back, and circled them. "It's a race. You know, as in *run?*"

Joe laughed. "Calm down, Wishbone."

Wishbone raced ahead again, sniffed the ground, then ran back toward the boys. He did that three times before they finally reached their camp site.

"Want some help?" He grabbed a corner of the folded up tent in his teeth and began tugging.

"No, Wishbone!" Joe removed the corner of the tent from Wishbone's mouth. "We've got to get the camp site set up before it gets dark."

"I get it. You need a supervisor. Okay. I'll lie right here and watch you." He dropped down. "Move the

camp site a little to the left, guys. It's better grass and softer ground. Take it from a professional."

When the boys had finally gotten the tent set up and the camp site organized, they stood back and admired their handiwork.

"So this is a pup tent," Wishbone said. "Well, I think you forgot to bring the door." Wishbone crawled inside with the boys. "I'll take the spot in the middle, Joe, between you and David." He sat down. "You know, so I can protect both of you at once—just in case there are any big, ferocious animals around." His wagging tail swished across the grass. "Bring on the pizza cookies! Bring on adventure!" Wishbone dropped his head and looked out through the tent flap. "Hey, did you guys hear something? Uh . . . Joe, it's getting dark. Can I be in charge of the flashlight?"

About Robert Louis Stevenson

Robert Louis Stevenson was one of the most popular writers of the late 1800s. He believed that stories should supply adventure for people who led ordinary lives. Two famous high-adventure novels that he wrote are *Treasure Island* and *Kidnapped*. Children, as well as adults, find these stories fun to read. Stevenson also wrote one of the most fascinating horror stories ever written— *The Strange Case of Dr. Jekyll and Mr. Hyde*.

Stevenson loved the open air, the sea, and adventure. He also loved to read, which was fortunate for him. In his youth, he suffered from a lung disease and spent a lot of time alone indoors. (Perhaps that was why he had such a wonderful imagination!) His lung disease eventually developed into tuberculosis, and he was forced to write many of his novels in a sickbed. For his reading material, he preferred books about Scottish history. He used Scotland as the background for many of his novels.

Stevenson was born in Edinburgh, Scotland, in 1850. Throughout his life, whenever he felt well enough, Stevenson left Scotland, traveling abroad in search of a warmer, drier place to live, in hopes of improving his health. He finally settled in the South Pacific, on the island of Samoa. Robert Louis Stevenson died unexpectedly in 1894, at the age of forty-four. He was working on a novel that was unfinished at the time of his death.

More than one hundred years later, Stevenson is still admired by readers, including Wishbone.

About *Kidnapped*

Robert Louis Stevenson wrote *Kidnapped* while he was very ill and homesick for Scotland. Like his main character, Alan Stewart, Stevenson longed to see the heather—a floral shrub found in Scotland. Perhaps that was why Stevenson wrote so convincingly about Alan's love of the Scottish Highlands.

In his youth, Stevenson loved reading about Scottish history; it eventually led to his becoming obsessed with his homeland. Another novelist once called him the "Scot of Scots." Stevenson's deep knowledge of the land and of the people of Scotland supplied the setting for many of his novels, including *Kidnapped*.

Although *Kidnapped* is a work of fiction, the story is woven around a real-life Scottish murder. In 1745, Colin Campbell—also known as the Red Fox—was shot to death in Appin.

Kidnapped was first published in 1886 in parts (May–July) in the magazine *Young Folks*. Because the story was long, Stevenson ended *Kidnapped* before the plot was finished. He finally completed the story, and in 1893 a sequel was published: *David Balfour*. Many people consider *Kidnapped* to be Stevenson's best novel.

About Vivian Sathre

Vivian Sathre spends a lot of time writing at her computer, so she loves it when she has a chance to sink her teeth into a good adventure story. *Kidnapped*, by Robert Louis Stevenson, was just such a story. Writing *Dog Overboard!*, based on *Kidnapped*, was a real treat for Vivian. It was pizza and ginger snaps all the way! She finds writing for Wishbone extremely enjoyable, maybe because they see eye to eye—or is that eye to knee?—on a lot of matters. They both enjoy a good book and a good snack. And Vivian, like Wishbone, likes to go for walks without a leash.

There is one subject on which Vivian disagrees with Wishbone—cats. She has two that she loves—a big, black, cuddly one named Jack; and a small Siamese named Rocky. Although Rocky walks and talks like a cat, he acts like a dog. He buries some of his toys under the sofa, and he chews others to bits. He loves a good scratch behind the ears, and his favorite game is tug-of-war. Vivian thinks Wishbone might even like Rocky, if he'd give him the chance!

Vivian has written a number of books for young readers, including picture books, chapter books, and books for middle-grade readers. *Dog Overboard!* is her second WISHBONE book. Her first was *Digging Up the Past*, based on "Rip Van Winkle," by Washington Irving.

Vivian lives in the Seattle, Washington, area with her husband, Roger, and their children.